The Watcher

The Watcher

Margaret Buffie

Kids Can Press

Kids Can Press acknowledges the support of the Ontario Arts Council, the Canada Council for the Arts and the Government of Canada, through the BPIDP, for our publishing activity.

Published in Canada by
Kids Can Press Ltd.
29 Birch Avenue
Toronto, ON M4V 1E2

Published in the U.S. by
Kids Can Press Ltd.
4500 Witmer Estates
Niagara Falls, NY 14305-1386

Edited by Charis Wahl
Cover designed by Marie Bartholomew
Map art by Jim Macfarlane
Interior designed by Stacie Bowes
Printed and bound in Canada by Webcom Limited

CM 00 0 9 8 7 6 5 4 3 2 1
CM PA 00 0 9 8 7 6 5 4 3 2

Selection from *The Mystic's Dream* by Loreena McKennitt appears courtesy of Quinlan Road Music Ltd. ©1994.

Canadian Cataloguing in Publication Data

Buffie, Margaret
        The watcher
ISBN 1-55074-829-7 (bound)   ISBN 1-55074-831-9 (pbk.)
I. Title

PS8553.U453W37 2000   jC813'.54 C00-930335-9
PZ7.B895Wa 2000

Kids Can Press is a Nelvana company

For my editor, Charis — ever the watcher

A clouded dream on an earthly night

Hangs upon the crescent moon

A voiceless song in an ageless light

Sings at the coming dawn

Birds in flight are calling there

Where the heart moves the stones

From *The Mystic's Dream* by Loreena McKennitt

Prologue

The owl flies high above the ground, wings whuffting softly in the muggy air. Below it, a wide quilt of amber, green and purple fields flashes by, the road winding through it like a gray ribbon. Along that ribbon, a small figure on a bicycle coasts toward Sweeney's bee farm away from the town of Bruide, a drab square some distance off. The owl allows the bicycle to skim past under it, then turns slowly, descends and skims silently behind.

The girl pedals quickly, her short white hair lifting away from her narrow face. As she reaches Sweeney's field, she raises one arm and waves. A man stops his work and waves back. The girl picks up speed again, avoiding the puddles from the late-night rainstorm and turns on to a narrower ribbon leading to the bee farm.

The owl swoops up, turns and glides into Sweeney's hayloft to wait for the darkness.

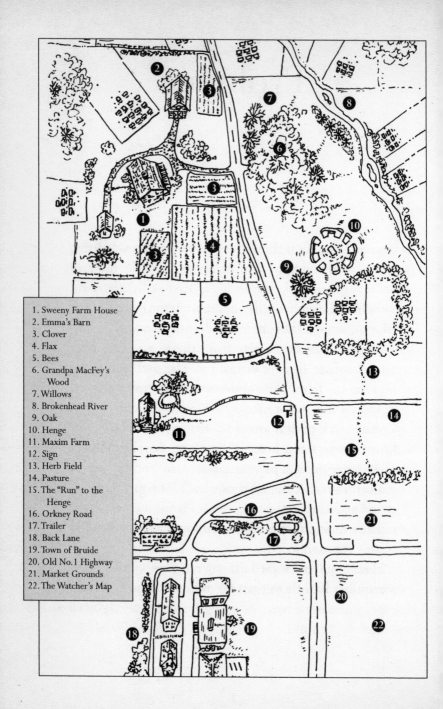

1. Sweeny Farm House
2. Emma's Barn
3. Clover
4. Flax
5. Bees
6. Grandpa MacFey's Wood
7. Willows
8. Brokenhead River
9. Oak
10. Henge
11. Maxim Farm
12. Sign
13. Herb Field
14. Pasture
15. The "Run" to the Henge
16. Orkney Road
17. Trailer
18. Back Lane
19. Town of Bruide
20. Old No. 1 Highway
21. Market Grounds
22. The Watcher's Map

1

I arrive home with the groceries and the first thing Mom says is, "I've found you a great summer job."

"But I don't want one!"

"Well, now you have one anyway."

I glare at her but she's gone back to hulling strawberries into a big white bowl. She pushes out her bottom lip and blows a curl of salt-and-pepper hair away from her eyes. One side of her sundress is pinned shut where she's ripped away the old zipper and hasn't gotten around to replacing it.

I take a deep breath. "You said as soon as school was over, you'd pay me to look after Summer and help out with the bees and all this other stuff that needs doing."

To make my point, I sweep one arm through the air, taking in the unpainted verandah we're standing on, the yard filled with Dad's junk, the tall windbreak of overgrown willow and the rolling prairie where rows of aging beehives zigzag across the clover field.

A rumble of thunder staggers toward us through the late-morning haze. Matches my mood exactly.

Mom presses one hand into the small of her back. "Winter —"

"I told you, Mom. I'm Emma. Not Winter. *Emma*."

Mom was born Esther Anne MacFey. Shortly after we arrived here, less than six months ago, she told me that when she married my dad she changed her name to Letonia. "Letonia comes from Leto — the Greek goddess of the sun and moon," she said, smiling and gazing off into some secret place behind her dark eyes. Apparently, she'd decided that everyone should acknowledge their ties to old Mother Earth, and chose a name that connected her to all the forces of nature.

So she can't complain that I changed my own name a week ago, can she? Or that I chose a quiet, reasonable one. Not like Winter. Or Summer. Or even worse, Letonia. At every new school I've ever gone to, I've had to put up with kids calling me "Icicle Face," "Snowcone Nose," "Ghostcicle" and just about every other stupid unoriginal name their little pea brains could think of. The combination of my ridiculous name, pale skin, white lashes and colorless cap of hair is always the cause of it. Well, now I'm plain old Emma. Let them make fun of *that*.

Mom smiles at me. "Are you aware that Emma means *grandmother*? Couldn't you have chosen a

name with more, I don't know ... more pizzazz ...
more *meaning*?"

A small voice chirps from the corner of the
verandah, "It suits her. She is an old grandmother.
And I, for one, will be *so* happy if she works all
vacation. Never gives me a break. Nag, nag, nag."

Summer is curled up on the rattan lounge,
reading. She gives me a grin and wrinkles her
nose the way she does when she's only teasing. I
can't help it — I smile. People always smile at my
little sister.

"That nagging got you a passing grade in math,
Summer, my love." Mom lifts the strawberry bowl
and heads into the house. I follow her yellow sundress down the humid hall.

"So what kind of job did you dig up for me?" I try
to keep my voice light, but anger fizzes in my chest.

Lately everything Mom does irritates me. In
fact, I seem to have trouble keeping *any* of my
feelings in balance. If I'm not cheesed off with
one of my parents, I'm worried about my little
sister's illness, and when I take a few minutes
away from worrying about that, I still feel all
jumbled up inside. Mom says she thinks it's
because my hormones are probably firing off all
at once. Apparently, I'm becoming a grown-up.
So I say, if this is what it feels like to become an
adult, who needs it?

Her voice penetrates my inner mutterings. "Albert Maxim, that fellow who's moved onto the old MacGregor farm, came by this morning and asked if I knew anyone who could look after his old dad for a few hours every day. It sounded like a good thing, so I suggested you."

I stare at her. "Are you kidding? You mean you said I'd baby-sit some old man I've never even laid eyes on?"

She holds the fruit under the gushing tap. "Wint— I mean, Emma, the old fellow is bedridden and only needs someone to give him lunch and read to him for a while each afternoon. What could be easier? You won't start until noon. Albert has to work in the fields if he's going to be ready for River Market weekends." She turns off the tap and muses, "You know, it's a strange thing. He got a market stall very quickly. He must be the first outsider they've let in that fast — actually, I think he's the *only* outsider they've *ever* let in. I mean, look at me — it took me months to convince them I could do as fine a product as my dad, and I was born here! But never mind all that ... what about this job? It's perfect, don't you think?"

I drop the groceries on the kitchen table with a thud. "I *think* it stinks, okay? I don't want to work away from home. You said I could help you! You *promised!*"

Mom sighs. "Well, I've given it some thought. I don't want you cooped up here until school starts again. You're too obsessed with Summer's illness — you hang around her like a little watchdog. It would be different if you had a *friend* — you'd be busy with your own stuff and less —"

I roll my eyes. "Oh please ... not that again?"

"Look, Win— Emma, I can't pay you to work on the farm. Not even an allowance. This job at the Maxims' ... well, I'd like you to take it. To help us out. There, I've said it. We need the money, okay?"

The kitchen is suffocatingly hot. Flies thump against the screen door. Thunder rumbles louder. I tug irritably at the damp collar of my shirt.

"It pays fifteen dollars an hour," Mom says, starting in on the fruit with a big metal masher. She eyes me with a half smile on her face.

"How much?" I squeak.

"Now, *that* got your attention. You could buy school clothes for the fall and ... lots of other things that Dad and I can't afford. Let's face it, your grandpa was just too old to keep the place updated and streamlined anymore. The inspector says I can't use the shop buildings until your dad upgrades them, so I'll have to keep the business small for this year at least. Every cent we've got is going toward getting it up and running again. You *know* that."

My mind seethes with the unfairness of it all. "If Dad would stop building that stupid pile of plastic in that *stupid* cow field and get going —"

"Come on now, that's his job. He'll work on the outbuildings in the fall. Right now he needs to do his art —"

I snort. She gives me a warning look.

"But *you* need my help, Mom! I need to be *here*."

"You've been a huge support, sweetie, but I can handle it now. Summer can sit right here at the table and make beeswax molds — and fix labels. *I'll* keep an eye on her. It will do you good to get away from fussing over her for a bit."

I sit on a hot sticky chair to think. Is she right? *Would* it be good to get away from the constant worry about Summer's strange attacks of sickness?

"Face it, Mom, she's a lot worse since we got here," I say. "She was supposed to get better!"

"We hoped she'd get better … that all this fresh air would make her stronger. It may take more time than we thought."

"But she *is* worse."

"Emma, she's seen doctor after doctor. What more can we do, your dad and I? And yes, I'm working day and night getting ready to finally make some money for us at the market, but I can *still* keep an eye on her. I'm her mother, after all!"

For the first time, I notice Mom's eyes are smudged with fatigue. She's been working so hard rebuilding the honey business. If she fails, maybe we'll have to move again — when Dad's finished making a mess in that field. I don't want Summer dragged around anymore. Besides, for the first time, I actually don't hate the place where we're living.

Taking this job is a chance to really help. How can I turn it down? Yet it will mean leaving Summer alone every day. Mom can promise all she wants, but she's way too busy to give Summer enough attention.

Mom's voice cuts through my misery. "At least try it out. Please?"

I grope for another way out. "Mom, what do you know about these Maxims?"

"Came here for the old man's health, that's all I know." She stops squashing the fruit and wipes her perspiring forehead with a paper towel. "Well … do I call the Maxim farm or not?"

I sigh. "And you *will* be able to keep an eye on Summer, being this busy and all?"

"Didn't I just say that?"

She looks so hopeful that a rush of affection makes me blurt out, "Oh … okay. I guess."

And with those four words echoing in the air, I know there's no going back.

2

This isn't the first time my parents have managed to mess up my neatly organized world. They don't mean to. Let's face it, they're just a couple of well-meaning time-bombs-of-annihilating-enthusiasm.

Like a few weeks before school ended — on careers day, a compulsory parent visit. Who waltzed into the classroom with a crown of wildflowers on her head and talked about organic beekeeping as one of the lost arts of the Wiccas? Who stood in front of a group of stunned kids and explained that bees have to be told all about important family events so that they don't get angry, and *then* who sat cross-legged on Mrs. Fant's desk and droned on and on about even more utterly mind-freezing, blindingly awful things, like "Did you know that bees are quiet and sober beings who don't like liars, cheats or lazy children?"

My mother. Letonia Sweeney — Earth Mother.

It was enough to make a *quiet and sober* person jump off a mountain — if there was one within a thousand miles of this barely rolling prairie. Definitely no point in jumping off one of the few hills out back by the river because I'd only land in my father's latest Work of Art.

I've always tried to keep secret the fact that my environmental artist father does things like wrap balloons in silver paper, string them through trees and call the whole mess "Models on Runway Number 2" or some equally goofy name.

If he'd been unleashed on my classmates, he'd have proudly told them that he was creating a copy of an ancient stone henge on a piece of our land across the road, not far from the farmhouse. I couldn't let him announce that bit of news. Without a mountain to jump off, I'd have had to dig a hole — somewhere in Ewan MacFey's cow field — big enough for me to hide out in for ten years at least.

Ewan MacFey is — was — my grandfather. He died a month before we moved here. I only met him once — well, twice really, but the first time I'd just been born, so of course I wasn't paying much attention. The other time was when I was seven. I remember him as small, square and very dark, with a thick beard. And he often wore white overalls and a hat with a flowing net attached to it. But I have one memory of him that couldn't possibly have happened. I see him standing in the clover field behind the farmhouse, sunlight bouncing off his white hat. When he turns to look at me, his beard is a swarm of glittering bees. See what I mean? Couldn't have happened.

Anyway, after he died, we drove here to Manitoba and Mom immediately took over the bee farm. After, that is, she went out to the hives that surround the farmhouse and Grandpa MacFey's old cow field and told the bees of their master's death. She explained to Summer and me that this was something she had to do or the bees would also die. For some reason, she's taken to remembering a lot of her father's old-world superstitions. And seems to actually believe them.

Summer was happy about the move right from the get-go. But then Summer's always happy despite being sick so much of the time. As for me, I decided I could just as easily live here as anywhere else. What did it matter? I've never felt as if I ever belonged in any of the other half-dozen places we've lived. Never made friends. Never fit in. Not even in my own family, really. I mean, they're all dark haired and dark eyed, while I look like I was left in a freezer too long — white on white. Icicle Face, that's me. Like a ghost from the other side.

I watch Mom finish squashing the fruit, humming softly, her stubby brown hands wrapped firmly around the handle of the masher. Have I done the right thing taking this job? I think so. Yet, listening to her off-tune warble, I'm suddenly swamped by a wave of sadness that makes it hard to breathe. My throat hurts from holding back the feeling that I want to cry. It's been happening more and more often lately, and like everything else going on inside me, I don't know why.

Mom takes her quiet trilling into the preparation room beside the kitchen and measures the strawberries into a deep, clean crock, then pours in honey from a number of huge, clear jars. Through the door I can see the rest of the ingredients for the farm's famous Honey-Blush Mead resting in bowls on the counter. The air is heavy with humidity and thick with the syrupy smell of crushed strawberries and sweet clover.

She comes back into the kitchen, washes her hands, then glances sharply at me. "You look peaky. You okay?"

I don't feel okay, but I nod. "When does this Albert Maxim want me to start?"

"Tomorrow." Mom reaches for a tartan carryall on the table. "Right now I'd like you to give this to your dad. He hasn't eaten properly in days."

Maybe a walk will take away this awful feeling inside.

Thunder grumbles louder. "Wear a rain jacket, sweetie," Mom says. "Sounds like it'll be coming down soon."

I put on one of the yellow slickers hanging beside the door and step out onto the stone stoop.

A cool breeze suddenly chases the heat out of the yard and lifts strands of hair off my hot forehead. A muttering cloud closes in overhead, turning the alfalfa field dark purple.

"Win— *Emma*. You'd better wait a bit," Mom says, her eyebrows crinkled. "I feel too much energy from those clouds. They're full of dynatron."

My mother speaks in perfectly sensible English most of the time but now and again lapses into *earth-speak*. It usually happens when she's *feeling something in the air*. With the weather, it's *dynatron* or *proton charges* or *electromagnetism*. With people, it's *energy* or *auras* or *intangible spirituality*.

"I'll be okay," I say, walking down the steps.

Through the screen door she calls, "Shouldn't you wait? That sky is boiling with electro-pulsations. I'd rather —"

"I won't be long."

Lately she's been getting sillier with all this psychic energy mumbo jumbo and I'm in no mood to listen to it. I march down the gravel driveway, past the barn, toward the peace and solitude of Grandpa MacFey's poplar wood.

3

The front of the bee farm faces the old Trans-Canada Highway — here it's just a two-lane road that winds its lazy way past small prairie towns and farmlands toward the forests and lakes of the Sandilands, about an hour east.

I sling the carryall over one shoulder and hike down the sloping driveway. One of the small bundles of inky clouds sweeps above my head, carrying with it an acrid electrical smell. As I approach the wood, the low mass catches on the treetops like a huge ball of steel wool and stops. Rain, for sure.

I cross the road quickly, drag open the rotting gate and trot into the shelter of the trees. In the strange half-light I can hear the rustle of leaves overhead. At least they offer a thick canopy that'll hold off most of the rain when it comes.

Generations of Grandpa MacFey's cows once cow-plattered their way through these poplars. Dad sold off the straggling remains of the herd right after the old man died. Now low-growing bunchberries, moss and patches of grass are slowly taking over the hard-packed dirt again. To my left, I can see the dull glint of water off the narrow channel of the Brokenhead River. On the other side of the river's willows is another bee field. The wood and the cow field are like an island ringed with hives.

Usually when I walk into the green coolness of Grandpa MacFey's little forest, I feel calm and happy. I like it more than any other place on Earth. Sometimes I cross the wood to the river and sit on its shady banks, watching turtles sunning on flat rocks or wading birds mincing their way down sandy shoals, looking for minnows. But for some reason, the wood feels different today — unfriendly, alien. I'm trying to work out what's wrong when something crashes overhead with a slash of light like a monstrous flashbulb. I fly backward, bang full force against a tree trunk and land on my backside in the dirt. In the unearthly silence that follows, thousands of blue flashing dots bounce in front of my eyes. I blink rapidly, trying to focus. Is that a figure — no — two figures shuddering toward me?

"Dad?" I gasp, but they don't answer.

Frightened, I lurch to my feet, lean against the tree and wait for the jiggling lights to melt away. When they do, there's no one in the wood but me and a strange unnerving silence.

I stagger to the opening that leads to Dad's field, the carryall banging heavily against my side. Smoke rises from the huge oak near his work area. Oh no! I fly past his sun tent rigged out of red-and-green parachute material and head straight for the smoke. When he dances out of the vapor, laughing with glee, I let out a whoosh of relief.

"Dad? W-what happened?"

"Emma! Lightning struck — again! Come and see! It's amazing."

He drags me to the huge oak that dominates the narrow field. Thin sheets of vapor spiral upward through the heavy air and tangle in the top branches. When I look up, my head thumps.

"Amazing! I couldn't have planned it better myself! I mean ... *look!*" he cries.

It's as if someone has taken a knife and sliced a narrow strip down the full length of the trunk. A coil of blackened bark lies curled at its base. The white of the oak's flesh is stark against the ancient crust of brown skin. The smell of sap and seared bark fills my nostrils. I touch the moist flesh and jerk my hand away. My fingertips are icy cold. If lightning did this to the tree, it would have killed Dad.

"You must have seen that black cloud!" I cry. "Why didn't you run for shelter?"

He flaps his hand at me. "I know, I know. But, Emma, remember I told you about the weird bolt of lightning that landed in this field during the last big storm? Remember — there was a shallow round depression and the hint of a rocky circle here? Remember?"

How could I forget? He took me to the field after he found the burn marks from the first lightning strike and showed me the so-called "circle of stones." All I could see was a jumble of tiny rocks in a rough circle. And the depression in the ground was just an ordinary dried-up watering hole for the cows.

Ignoring my frown, he continues eagerly, "It's like the place is attracting some power. First one lightning strike and now another — and this time, what does it do? Hits the tree! I'm so happy your mom suggested this field." He sobers immediately. "Listen, Emma, don't tell her about the lightning. For some reason she's been getting edgy about my project lately, and you know how she's always going on about portents and atmospheric warnings."

"Okay, I won't tell her. But, Dad, lightning *has* been known to strike a place more than once. Next time it could hit *you*. Maybe Mom's right —" I stop and save my breath because now that he has my promise not to blab, he's gone off into his own fantasy again.

"Look! Right down the trunk," he says, "and *then* all the way to the very center of my henge! The very *exact* center!"

He lurches around me in a heavy-footed dance. He's right, though. Where the oak's trunk meets the soil, a blackened groove has sliced across the earth to the center of the shallow bowl where he's been digging. Bits of grass and small plants still smolder.

"Like a branding iron," I whisper, and shiver in a cold breeze that carries with it a flutter of raindrops.

"Walk its length … you'll see what I mean," Dad says. "Now I'm *completely* convinced I made the right choice putting my henge here! I'm going to call it Brute Energy of Bruide. There's something here, Emma, some power — some energy that …"

I stop listening and walk alongside the sooty groove toward the center of the henge, fighting pinpricks of irritation. Then, like I do every other day, I shrug and give up with a sigh. He'll never change.

When Mom decided it wouldn't interfere with the surrounding bee fields and gave Dad permission to use the land, he announced he was going to build a big stone circle similar to one in England called Stonehenge, right there in Grandpa MacFey's cow field. He tried to involve the whole family in his excitement. He told us how Stonehenge was made by dragging walloping boulders into a huge circle. Some people think it was a place for human sacrifices to unknown gods; others think it was an ancient observatory. A few even think it was a UFO landing site … believe me, other theories are even weirder.

So, Dad became obsessed with stone circles, researching everything he could about them. "It's amazing how many remains of stone circles and henges there are all around the globe," he told me one day after surfing the Net on his rented computer. "And you know what? After a lot of thinking, I've decided that Stonehenge is way too famous for me to copy — too … commonplace now. So I've finally decided on a not-so-famous stone circle called Bruide Henge, in Scotland. Wild. Unknown. Perfect!"

"Bruide?" I said. "Like our town?"

"Yes! Neat, huh? Actually, your mom inadvertently gave me the idea. She said the founders of our Bruide came from an area surrounding an ancient stone circle in northern Scotland. So I looked it up and there it was on the Net! I'm going to do *my* henge in modern materials — Plexiglas and treated wood. We need new monoliths in Canada. Places of mystery and magic. It'll be *amazing*."

"Amazing" is Dad's favorite word, for anything from a chocolate cake to a Mars space probe. My father thinks everything is amazing. He's a big kid, and the whole world is his very own playpen. It gets tiring, believe me. Like having a geriatric Peter Pan in the family.

I watch him prance around the smoldering site, his beard jeweled by drops of rain, looking like a long-legged elf performing a pagan dance.

"So what do you think?" he crows. "Isn't this lightning strike *amazing*? Doesn't it fit the name for my circle perfectly?"

"Brute Energy of Bruide? I guess ... Dad, look, you don't really believe there's some kind of special energy here, do you? You do know it's just a cow field with a damaged oak tree, right?" He needs to be settled down a bit — he's higher than the smoke in the branches overhead.

"There are more things in heaven and earth, Emma, than are dreamt of in your philosophy," he says, smiling.

"Huh?"

"Shakespeare. Hamlet. Never mind. Come here. Look!"

I sigh and walk around pieces of Plexiglas and chunks of wood lying in piles on the ground. He's cleared some of the low brush and dug a circular trench to mark out his henge. He points at a jagged hole in the center of the hollow. I step forward, and as the sole of my shoe touches the long slice of seared earth, a sizzle of electricity buzzes into my toes. Another thing that my father is good at — if I'm not really watchful — is making *my* imagination go off-kilter. This is stupid. I'm letting his silliness infect me again. Sometimes when this happens, part of me wants to go along with him, but this time, for some reason, I know I have to stifle it. I back away a few steps and put my hands on my hips.

"Did you dig that hole?" I ask, accusingly.

He grins. "No, I didn't. The strike did it. And it's really deep. Come on, Emma. You've got to admit it. *That's* amazing!"

He's off again, soaring into magic land. Absolutely no idea what it's like to live in the real world.

"I can make use of that hole — as a dolmen — a burial cist," he says.

That stops me. "A *burial* cist? You're going to bury something here?"

"Don't worry, Emma. Nothing alive — or dead for that matter. No … something very small — and symbolic — like a carved stone or something. I haven't decided yet. But over it I'll put a pedestal-type table — they call it a socle — and on that I'll put the chunk of amethyst crystal I found half buried in the dirt last week." He stops talking and stares across the field. "Hey, there's that kid from town again. He's always hanging around. Got someone with him this time."

Two figures dressed in black rain ponchos, their heads uncovered, stand silently by the barbed wire fence. A boy my age. And an older woman with a mop of black hair. They're holding the bridles of two horses. Was it them in the wood? If so, why didn't they say anything to me?

"What's *he* doing here?" I mutter.

"Do you know them?"

"The kid was in my class. If I was you, I'd tell him to get lost."

"Why?"

"Because I don't trust him. That's why."

"Just like that, Emmy? He's obviously interested in what I'm doing. Never mind, I've got work to do." He wanders off, muttering about a measuring tape.

I glare at the silent couple across the field. Tom Krift arrived in town during the last few weeks of school and sat silently at the back of the class, glowering at no one in particular but making everyone uneasy. He's big and broad with a battered face and spiky black hair. He always wears black jeans, work boots, a white T-shirt, a leather strap around his thick neck and two wide copper bracelets on his wrists. Even Mrs. Fant studiously ignored him, and I could see he made her nervous, too. He actually spoke to me in quite a decent tone when we had to work on a final science project together, and then one day he grabbed my arm and examined the birthmark on my wrist, his thumb sliding over the two mauve shapes. His hand was warm, my arm tingled, and something loosened and dropped softly inside me. But when I looked up, his dark eyes were examining my face with such intensity that I yanked my arm away. Since then, I've been wary around him.

The distant figures turn and climb up the side of the ditch onto the road, the horses following. Dad has already forgotten them and is on his knees by the hole, measuring tape in hand.

"I'll put your lunch in the tent," I say. "I'm heading home."

"Don't you want to help me measure this? It's fascinating. It really is."

"Don't think so, Dad. I'd only point out things you don't want to hear."

He grins. "You always keep my feet firmly on the ground, kiddo. Hey, take this home, will you?" He holds up a plastic bag that sags with something heavy.

"What is it?"

"The chunk of amethyst. I won't need it for a while yet. But don't put it near your pillow." He grins.

"Why not?"

"Because the amethyst is the crystal of dreams — don't want you having weird ones. Also, don't leave town without it, because held or worn in plain sight, it wards off highwaymen."

"Oh gee, thanks for telling me. I was worried about highwaymen," I say, and he cackles like mad.

It's starting to spit heavily now. I make a face at him, take the bag, drop his lunch off in the tent, tighten my hood strings under my chin and retrace my way through the trees. The wood is quiet, the rain sifting lightly through the leaves. My head feels better and I'm hungry. I open the rotting gate and climb up onto the bank, squelching through thick mud and old cow dung. Just as my foot hits the road, a green truck roars by and sprays me from head to toe with brown water.

I shout, "Creep!" and almost fall over when a deep voice behind me asks, "Are you okay?"

Sheltered by an overhanging silver willow, Tom Krift and the strange woman sit very still on their horses. With their black poncho hoods up, they look like ancient monks from a storybook.

"A b-bit wet, that's all," I stammer.

The woman is about Mom's age, heavy and dark like Mom, except her hair is jet black, not salt and pepper. I glance quickly at Tom Krift, but he's leaning down adjusting a stirrup. The woman sits easily on her horse, a half smile never leaving her face. Then she makes a clucking sound and the horse surges toward me, its hooves clattering heavily on the old tarmac.

I skitter across the road. When I reach the other side, I look back, but a sudden curtain of rain washes heavily across my face, momentarily blinding me. When I clear it from my eyes, the horses and riders are gone.

4

I run up the outside stairs of the barn to my room.
I toss Dad's plastic bag toward my straw bed, but
the handle hooks on my little finger and the bag falls
short, landing on the floor with a loud crack.

I peek inside. A small piece of amethyst has
broken off the larger one. Darn and double darn! I
grimace and pull both out. The larger chunk is dull
and cloudy, the smaller piece is about as long as my
index finger, a five-sided slice of clear purple.
There's a dusting of powdery residue in the bottom
of the bag.

Dad was so excited when he dug up the thing
last week. Amethyst isn't found around here, but
way off in southern Ontario. So what was it doing
half buried in Grandpa MacFey's cow field?, he
asked. But of course we didn't know. Or care much
either. I put the larger chunk back into the bag and
the smaller piece on my night table. With luck, Dad
won't notice the damage.

Throwing my rain slicker aside, I lie down on
the bed and watch a daddy longlegs mince its way

across the wooden ceiling. I tap my finger against the wall and its thread-legs suddenly go into high gear, bouncing its button body toward a hiding place near the eaves. That's what Tom Krift and that woman just did to me. Made me scuttle for home by tapping on a hidden wall inside me, making me feel exposed and afraid. Of what, I have no idea, but my heart is still a bit shaky. And I'm angry, too. Angry that I let them unnerve me.

I concentrate on allowing my own little hiding place to calm me. When we first came to live on the farm, Summer and I were each allowed to choose our own private space — off-limits to everyone else. Summer chose the tiny sunroom that opens off her bedroom. I picked this space above the barn. I liked the idea of being perched up here with a wide-open view of the yard — and the comings and goings of my family.

I think Grandpa MacFey must've planned a storeroom up here, marking off a small square room with insulated wood walls and a plank floor. There's even a trap door in the side wall that opens on to a wide beam overlooking the cavernous barn. Dad says the little door is probably for easy access to the cross beams in case they ever need repairing.

The week we arrived, I took some boards that were lying around in the barn and made bookshelves, which I stacked with my favorite books — along with mosquito coils and a couple of good flashlights. I even hauled up some sweet hay and made a mattress on the floor, covering it with an old quilt, then my duvet and two plain pillows. I also found an old wooden icebox in one of the sheds and now I use it as a cupboard, to keep the mice away from my hoard of junk food. Dad's promised to buy me a heater for the winter months. It's not perfect, but it suits me just fine.

There are windows in my room, too — a small one that faces the road and a large one that overlooks the house. I made a window seat under the big one. Dad calls it my lookout post and he waves to me every night before he goes to bed.

The best part is being able to have an uncluttered space. Mom sees no point in putting anything away — "It'll just get taken out and used again." The only place Mom keeps pristine clean is the temporary honey-preparation room off the kitchen. She has to, or the inspector will take away her license.

The day I finished my room in the barn, I announced I didn't need the one in the house. I told them it was too small — I *couldn't* tell them that it was because I wasn't able to see the yard from the room's lone window — and I needed to keep an eye on who came to the farm. Don't ask me why. It's just something I have to do.

My tummy grumbles, reminding me I haven't eaten since breakfast. I cross the yard under a dank gray sky toward the blare of rock music and two wailing voices. Through the screen door I can see

Mom swaying her hips to the music while Summer conducts. Neither can hold a tune, even if their lives depended on it, but they don't care — if it's loud, it's good. I want to join in, but I can't. That same deep sadness returns and tightens my throat. I grope for the door handle and it snaps shut behind me just as the music ends.

"Oh good, you're back," Mom says. "Dad okay?"

I nod, kick off my duck boots, but keep my rain slicker on. I open the fridge, about to take out salad makings, when Mom adds, "Albert Maxim wants you to start today. Now, actually."

I stare at the green onions in my hand. "And I suppose you said yes?"

"I was about to come and get you."

"She was going to send me," Summer says, "but I had another fall-out."

A sickening jolt strikes me in the stomach and my appetite vanishes. Summer always calls her strange bouts of weakness "fall-outs." They've been attacking her since she was a baby, but they're definitely getting worse. An army of specialists hasn't been able to find out what's wrong. Most say it's allergy based and she'll probably outgrow it. All they do is give her bottles of pills and piles of inhalers. None help. Most make it worse.

Mom and Dad even took her to a few "alternative" doctors — the kind some people call holistic healers and others call quacks. After trying no-yeast, no-dairy, no-sugar, no-wheat and even no-fat diets, Summer remains exactly the same.

Dad gently teases her, calling her attacks "The Victorian Vapors," but I know that he and Mom are as bewildered as the doctors. And me, I'm always on the lookout for something that will finally tell us why she's forced to spend so much time in bed having difficulty breathing, her body as weak as a baby mouse's.

Like me, Summer was born here on the farm. A few weeks before she was due, my parents brought me to stay with Grandpa MacFey. They intended on going into Winnipeg two weeks before Mom's due date so she could be close to a city hospital. But the day after we got here, she suddenly went into labor. I found out later that the very same thing had happened when I was born — they didn't think it could happen a second time. The district doctor was in bed with the flu, so Grandpa MacFey had to call the local midwife. Despite my frantic pleading, I was dragged off to stay with the midwife's family until it was over.

Hours later, when I finally gazed down at the rumpled little face of my baby sister, I was filled with such a fierce protectiveness that I even pushed away my grandpa when he got too close. It worried Mom, but the midwife just laughed and said she wished more older sisters were as protective.

I was seven years old that summer when my sister was born, too young to explain my overwhelming need to protect her. Now, nearly sixteen, I still can't explain it. It's as if, somehow, I'm the one who will have to keep Summer safe — my parents just aren't going to be up to it when the time comes. The time for what? I don't know. I just know I have to be on guard.

Mom hadn't seemed very happy to have a new baby. She cried all the time, while Dad hovered around her, wringing his hands and trying to cheer her up. I stuck close to my sister's crib except when Dad chased me outside to get some fresh air.

Once, I walked by the kitchen and overheard Grandpa MacFey and the midwife talking. I guess she was there to give Mom a pep talk or something. She didn't look very happy, either. She was standing with her head down as Grandpa MacFey said in an urgent voice, "You've done the right thing, Ina. You've done what was expected of you. My grandchild will go to a better place. She will be honored, even revered. We're part of something bigger than either of us. We must protect —" Then he caught sight of me and stopped talking. The look he gave me was scary, as if he'd never seen me before. Then he cleared his throat, smiled and waved me away. I backed off, but stood in the hallway long enough to hear him say, "Now, *that* one is doing what she's supposed to do. You did the right thing there, too, Ina. Let's get you home. I'll watch over my daughter and her family."

The woman sighed and said, "You're right, of course, Ewan MacFey. But the old ways are not easy."

Their voices were cut off when the back door banged shut. I heard his truck start up.

Upstairs I found my white-faced mother packing our bags. Dad, looking bewildered, carried them downstairs, made me get in the back seat of the car, pushed the baby's car bed in beside me and helped Mom into the front — and we drove away from Grandpa MacFey's farm. I don't know if she said good-bye to her father, but I do know we never saw the old man again.

And now, here we are, living in his house. I look at Mom and wonder. Why on earth did she come back to the farm when she was so unhappy the last time we were here?

"You'd better get a move on," she says. "And don't look so worried — you'll do a good job at the Maxims'."

A bristly anger makes me snap, "Do you mind if I have something to eat first?"

"Albert Maxim said lunch could be included."

"I'm not sure I want this job," I mutter testily.

"Just try it for one week, okay?" she says wearily. "Please?"

Summer looks up from her book. "You should go, Emmy. You *need* money for some new clothes. I'll be okay. Honest."

"Bet they'll try to feed me bologna sandwiches or something equally disgusting."

When I was eight years old, I decided — after seeing a nature film at school — that I would no longer eat anything that had eyes. I've tried and tried to talk my family into going vegetarian, but "Earth Mom" claims that people have been meat eaters forever, and that's how nature made us. I say that nature gave us brains to change things, too.

"I suppose you didn't mention I don't eat dead animals, Mother?"

"As a matter of fact, I did, *Daughterrr*," she trills, pouring beeswax into her little beehive molds. She'll sell them at the market, just like her father did for all those years. "Listen, don't be put off by Albert Maxim. He's very — um — enthusiastic."

"Oh, greeeat." I stuff the onions back in the fridge. "*Enthusiastic*."

"You need some enthusiasm, Emmy," Summer says. "Your world is so ... so *boring*."

"Wearing clown clothes doesn't make *you* less boring," I counter, pointing at her bright red-and-pink striped T-shirt and lime green pants. She sticks out her small chest, smoothes down her shirt and grins. I grin back.

"Do you want me to drive you?" Mom wipes her hands on a towel.

"No, I'll take the bike. The rain's stopped for a while."

"Okay. Here, give Mr. Maxim some honey, honey" — an old joke she keeps repeating, but what can a person do? "And thank you, Emma," she adds. "It'll work out, you'll see. And it will really *really* help."

I counter with a slightly exaggerated sigh and slip the jar of honey into my pocket. "I just hope these men aren't bank robbers or something, hiding out on that old farm." I only partially regret it when Mom's forehead creases with worry.

Summer cries. "Hey! Maybe they'll take you hostage, Emma! Wouldn't that be neat? Some excitement in your *beige* little life?"

I offer casually, "At least I don't waste mine reading baby romance books."

I slam through the door just as Summer's latest Sweet Dreams paperback bangs against the screen. At the gate leading onto the old highway, I stop the bike and look back. I don't feel right leaving. Mom appears on the verandah and waves. I wave back listlessly, then aim my wheels toward the Maxims' farm.

5

The rain has turned their road into pea soup. How the heck am I supposed to wheel down that? To my right, a hand-painted sign looms through the haze. "The Green Alchemist — Natural Herbs, Essential Oils and Aromatic Extractions." Doesn't alchemy have something to do with magic or witches or something? Great. I'm going to end up working for some back-to-the-land oddball from the city. The dull, staid, hardworking people from the farms and town around here won't put up with anything this weird for long. Mom said that outsiders have always been carefully checked over before being accepted, and so far, they've only been accepted by marrying someone from town. How the heck did Albert Maxim rent this place and get a stall at the market, when Mom — who is from an old local family — had to work so hard to get in? I grin. Everyone in Bruide thinks Mom and Dad are a bit weird. Wait until they see this sign.

Behind the mist, the sun hangs like a fuzzy yellow tennis ball. I can just make out a large farmhouse standing like a distant block of gray ice. Somewhere on the second floor is the sick old man I'm supposed to baby-sit every afternoon all summer. Probably a senile skeleton with grabby hands. Why oh why did I agree to take this stupid job before I checked out the place? Mom definitely worked one of her premium guilt trips on me. Sucker punched.

The loud *kawoo* of a horn lifts me right off the road. The bike falls to the ground, landing with a dull squelch. When I whirl around, an ancient green truck is almost touching my legs. How come I didn't hear *that* drive up? It looks exactly like the one that splashed me an hour ago.

A huge straw hat pokes out of the driver's window. "Halloo!" a voice cries. "I hope you're Winter Sweeney."

"I'm Emma Sweeney," I growl back. "Not Winter … Emma!"

"Oops! Must have misheard your mother." The door swings open with a crunking sound and a skinny man dressed in a dull green shirt, oversized khaki pants and heavy brown sandals takes off his hat, grabs my hand, shakes it wildly up and down, then stands back to gaze at me intently. My hand hurts from the wringing, never mind the huge gold rings on his fingers.

"So this is you, is it?"

"If you mean Emma Sweeney," I say stiffly, "then yes this is her — *I* — *me*."

He smiles and runs his hand through his thick thatch of reddish brown hair. "Somehow I pictured you much younger, but then ... well ... that wouldn't make sense would it? How old are you exactly?"

"Almost sixteen."

"But you *do* read?"

I pull myself up to my not-very-great height. "Of course I can read!"

"And do you play games?"

"What kind?"

He taps one finger on his chin. "Oh I don't know ... board games?"

"My father taught me chess."

"Your father? That would be Mr. Sweeney, who toils so creatively in that field near our land? Chess ... yes ... close enough. Come on, let's see what *he* makes of you. This oughtta be good."

With that, he loads my muddy bike into the back of the truck and we fishtail down the boggy track, spin around a hairpin turn and slide to a stop in front of the stone house.

A couple of fresh flower beds have been dug around the front steps. Maybe a bit of color will make the place look less like a stone box. Barn swallows fly out from under the wide eaves of the house and slice through the thick air, chinking like tiny change purses.

I hand him the jar of honey. "My mom sent this."

"Aaah. Nectar of the gods, eh? Thank her for me. I'm Albert Maxim, but no doubt you've worked that out — you look like a reasonably intelligent little being. You'll give Poppy a run for his money, I hope!" He giggles and minces to the door.

I hesitate. If this is the son, what's the old man going to be like? Once I'm in the front hall, my eyes widen. The walls are painted with thick vines — a mix of drab greens and red-browns that slide across a dull orange background. They look uncannily real, as if they could twist right out of the wall, grab me and suck me in.

Albert flaps his bony hand in the air. "I had a bit of time on my hands waiting for my seeds to sprout. Then I had to wait *again* for the dim-witted owner of the nursery on the other side of town to get in the plants I ordered. The walls in this old place were ugly and cracked, so I decided to brighten them up. Do you like my painting?"

He calls this *bright*? "It's — umm — very interesting," I say, when what I really mean is spectacularly creepy.

"It takes getting used to, I suppose," he says, looking hurt. "But it reminds me of where we live — uh — used to live. Come on, you can get started by carrying Poppy's lunch up to him. Have you eaten?"

"Yes," I lie. I wouldn't trust anything this oddball offered me.

"Oh good," he says and vanishes down the dark hall.

I glance into each room as we pass by. Every square inch of the walls is smothered with huge plants and trailing vines. I'm surprised the vines aren't crawling across the floor, they look so real.

When we walk into the kitchen, monster vegetable gourds roll across the ceiling like dark clouds, while purple cabbages and squash as big as pumpkins and pumpkins as big as tractor tires burst out along the walls. Even the cupboards are smeared in vegetation.

"Too much?" he asks.

I shake my head and try to smile sincerely, all the while thinking ... too much? ... how about *completely insane*?

Oddly enough, with his reddish hair and dun green clothes, Albert fits in perfectly, while I feel like a small white moth who's somehow fluttered into a giant's root cellar by mistake. Roots being the operative word here.

In the middle of a table — madly painted with bean vines bristling with huge pods — sits a full tray of food. Carrot and potato salads, cheeses, crackers, half a dozen slices of whole wheat bread, pots of what look like mayonnaise, mustard and butter, and a large glass bowl of shelled nuts covered with something oily. The whole room is thick with the odor of garlic, onions and a spicy smell that makes my mouth water.

"You sure you aren't hungry?" Albert asks.

I shake my head.

"Do you think you can lift this big tray? If it's too heavy, I'll have to make up two smaller ones each day. He doesn't like waiting for his food, but ... well, need's be, as they say."

I stare at the tray. "This is all for one person?"

Albert laughs. "Too heavy?"

"I think I can make it in one trip."

"Just don't! *Trip* that is." Albert snickers at his lame joke.

I hoist the tray. "Lead the way," I say in the firm I-won't-take-any-more-silliness voice that I use on my family.

He grins. He has a long wiffly nose and chestnut brown eyes, and his skin is thick with freckles that look as if they've been spatter-painted on. I can't tell his age, but he's younger than my parents — maybe in his late twenties. He wriggles his eyebrows and I realize I'm staring.

"Shall we?" He walks toward the far wall and opens a door that blends in so well with the crush of branches and leaves, I didn't even notice it was there.

As I pass through the doorway, my scalp tightens and a bewildering surge of dread shoots straight through my body. I fight it down and concentrate on keeping the tray from falling. Albert's paintbrush has been very busy here, too. Now I know what Alice felt like in the rabbit hole. Roots as big as my arm twist out of sooty soil like crusty brown snakes. I can almost smell the dank damp dirt. I'm so distracted and unnerved, I bang the tray on the wall and skin my knuckles. Just when I'm sure I'm going to drop the old man's lunch, we reach the top of the stairs and Albert Maxim opens a heavily varnished door with a flourish.

"Enter, those who dare," he sings.

I follow him into a dim room. The strong odor of cloves and a deep earthy smell mingle in the air. Against the far wall, propped up in the middle of an enormous bed piled high with embroidered pillows and surrounded by mounds of books and papers, sits a very old, very bald, very fat man dressed in bronze-colored silk pajamas. Rolls of pale flesh hang from a vast chin. Two piggy eyes blink at me before one weighty arm lifts off the bed and a mammoth pink hand with sausage fingers waves me closer. The fingers are covered in gold rings like Albert's, and there's a thick gold band on each wrist.

"Ahh. The new recruit for our game," the creature wheezes. "Was that you making that terrible racket on the stairs?"

"Th-the tray is heavy," I stammer, lowering it with a clatter on the table beside him. He pulls it forward and begins eating with noisy gulping slurps, all the while eyeing me with amusement.

I take in the rest of the room with quick furtive glances. The window that faces the driveway is covered with heavy green curtains. A small lamp highlights the huge bed. It has a giant carved headboard of acorns and oak leaves and four enormous acorn posts with a swag of embroidered greenish gray fabric looped from post-tip to post-tip. Almost everything else in the room is some variety of brown — the walls and rug a rich dark chocolate, the mass of crumpled damask bedcovers a mix of cinnamon and nut browns.

I can't see Albert and feel a flutter of panic, but find him sitting in semidarkness on a high-backed chair on the other side of the bed — a narrow table between him and the fat man. On it is a board game with ornately carved pieces. I can make out a kingly figure, a scattering of smaller beings, one that looks like a serpent, as well as numerous pieces shaped like trees and curious-looking buildings, all placed in various spots around the board.

"Is that some sort of chess?" I ask Albert, trying not to listen to the old man's disgusting noises.

"It's rather like it, I suppose," he says. "I made this set myself out of gromand's teeth."

Gromand's teeth? Is Albert Maxim a bit crazy? Is that why he paints the indoors to look like the outdoors? The fat man gives him a piercing look over fleshy nostrils, but Albert stands up, smiles complacently and says, "I've simply got to get back to my work, Emma dear."

I don't want to spend one more second with this monster who squashes and snuffles his food like an enormous hog, and it must show because Albert croons, "I fear she doesn't like it here, Poppy darling. Perhaps she's a wee bit afraid of you." His eyes shine with laughter. "Her antennae may be on a bit crooked, but her instincts are working."

"I'm not afraid of him," I say bravely, but my effort ends in a small squeak.

"Talking about me as if I'm not even in the room," wheezes the old man. "And I don't like it, I say, I do *not* like it. I can't help the way I eat, so you can turn that nose of yours right back into position, Little Sparrow."

A hot flush creeps up my neck. He actually read my mind.

Albert says, "Oh, come on, Poppy, she —"

The old man holds up a hand and snarls, "Don't even talk to me, Albert. It's too late, after what you've done! I can't see how this one can do much, after all —"

"Poppy!" Albert cries. "Think!" He turns to me with a smile like sticky syrup and says, "Run to the kitchen like a dear and get Poppy the glass of iced tea I left in the fridge."

I head downstairs quickly, not wanting to miss the argument because it seems to be about me. I can't find the fridge at first and shake my head when I realize he's painted all over that, too. Man, he *must* have been bored. I grab the huge glass mug of iced tea, climb the rabbit's hole stairway again and sneak up to the door.

The old man is snarling again. "How many times do I have to tell you, it was a waste of time bringing her here — a waste of time! All we have to do is guide the child —"

"You *know* you'll have to test your little minder, *Father dearest*," Albert says. I can hear the smile in his voice. "We won't know unless you do. Like you said yesterday, we're going to be here a few more days at least. Even though I'd leave now if I could."

"Yes, yes, all right! Where is the girl?" he growls, then bellows, "GIRL!"

That makes me scuttle into the room. I blurt out, "Are you going to give me some sort of test? For what?"

Albert laughs. "I told Poppy you like board games. He wants a good opponent. I just told him he'd have to test you out, that's all."

Somehow I know he's lying. Yet it seems to make sense with what I heard. Even so, I say quickly, "I think maybe — I'll just go outside for a few minutes and get some air, okay?" And grab my bike and — promise or no promise — take off for good.

Albert leaps in front of me. "Oh no you don't! I'm paying you good money to look after my trouble-some parent, and look after him you will! I've got to get back to work. Your mother promised!"

He gently leads me to the chair he vacated and presses on my shoulder until I sit. Then, hands on hips, he stares at the old man. "Well, Poppy, can I trust you to behave?"

The old man frowns ferociously, then resets his face into a sickening smile — a gruesome stump-toothed event. "Never you mind us, Sparrow," he says. "We've always been at each other's throats — ever since we were pups."

Albert whirls one finger at his temple.

He's right. The old man's crazy. They both are.

Poppy continues as if he hasn't said anything odd. "We'll play Fidchell and have a chin-wag. I promise not to yell at you, Sparrow. It's really not in my nature. How about getting a nice drop of cordial for Sparrow and me, Albert? Then you can leave us."

Albert goes to a table against the wall and pours red liquid from a bottle into two tall green glasses.

"Remember, Poppy dear, don't keep our little minder here past six o'clock," he warns, and before I can say a word, he's gone.

6

"Here!" Poppy lifts a huge mauve-blotched arm and wiggles his fingers at me. "Pay attention, Sparrow. I'm going to give you the basics of the game. When you come back tomorrow perhaps you will know enough to *attempt* to reach the goal before me. I play the king."

Why am I not surprised? "What's the goal?"

"You must watch over and protect three game tokens. You and your little band have to reach the Island of the Silver Cloud ...," he points at a small silvery land mass in a painted sea, "... before the king — that's me — and my players. Understand so far?"

I nod. "Yes, I understand."

"Fine. Now, when I capture you and your players, I win. If I *don't* capture you, but make it to the island first, well, then I win, too — because you can't get on to the island when I'm occupying it, I can claim your capture — checkmate you, so to speak, and the game is mine."

"And I win if I get to the island first, right?" I ask.

"Yes," he says matter-of-factly, "but you won't, of course. Now, here are the various moves."

I frown and concentrate on what movement each of the pieces on the wooden board is allowed. The whole time, Poppy eyes me intently. It makes me uncomfortable and self-conscious, like knowing you're being watched by a hidden camera in a convenience store. Before long, though, I'm too involved in the game to care.

The basic goal is fairly simple, but the moves are definitely confusing. The king is the largest piece on the board. He and his band of soldiers must try to chase me down through tiny towns and forests — herding me to the king's castle, where he can capture me. My job is to get my people past various magical beings and strange beasts to the far side of the board, where the small island lies. Once there we'll be safe. And win. My four pieces are made up of a small white figure with large eyes and three even smaller curiously shaped pieces with long cloaks and hidden faces. The good thing for me is that, while the king may have twenty soldiers, as the tiny white creature I have some magical powers he doesn't have.

We play for ages, and just as I am finally getting the hang of it, a fat arm sweeps the pieces onto the bedcovers.

"Hey!" I cry.

"Never mind!" wheezes the old man. "You'll do. You could possibly — and I say *possibly* — be a worthy opponent. But be prepared. It gets harder, girl. I was holding back of course. We'll play every day." For just a split second, I'm sure I see the flash of another gruesome grin cross his face, but it's followed quickly by a dark sadness that looks as phony as his grin. "I don't suppose you really want to come back, do you? Go, Sparrow. Come only if and when you want."

"I'll stay," I say, and surprise myself by meaning it. This visit hasn't turned out too bad. Besides, I really liked the game, feeling at times as if I was actually running through the woods keeping track of my players and a close eye on the sly and devious king. I look forward to playing it again.

He nods solemnly. "Well then, perhaps now you might read to me." He rummages around in the pile of papers on his bed and holds up a dark green book.

"David Copperfield by Charles Dickens," I say. "I read this last year right after they made a TV film about it. It's hard to read in places — the sentences aren't shaped like modern writing, but it's good."

"Not modern writing, eh?" he says with a wheezy chuckle. "Still, if you already know it, then you should have no trouble putting some feeling into it. They've gone and made my eyes too weak to read such small print. I can't …" He waves a hand at me. "Never mind, let's get on with it."

I open the cover and begin reading. "Whether I shall turn out to be the hero of my own life, or whether that station will be held by anybody else, these pages must show."

7

I read out loud, with sips of the tart red drink to see me through. The old man pays close attention for a while, but then, muttering something about "very little action," he suddenly starts snoring. I'm relieved, as my throat has become dry and scratchy. I finish the sentence I started, "But he had these peculiarities: and at first they frightened me, though I soon got used to them."

I close the book. Despite *his* peculiarities, I've pretty much got used to Poppy Maxim, too. I check my watch. Exactly 5:59. I put the book on the side table, lift the much lighter tray and tiptoe to the door.

"Will you come back?" his wheezing voice calls plaintively from the bed.

I nod.

"Good." And the snoring begins again in earnest.

When I reach the kitchen, Albert is at the stove stirring something that smells green and vinegary. "Aaah, there you are, Emma. I just finished work myself."

"You were outside in all this mud and rain?"

"Oh no! I was in the herbarium today. Not that mud and rain ever stopped *me*."

"Herbarium? Does that have anything to do with being an alchemist, like on your sign?"

Albert laughs. "Alchemy has to do with putting base metals together to make gold. I put that name on our sign for fun — I see myself as a sort of alchemist of plants, you might say."

"What's an herbarium?"

"I'll show you."

He opens a door — smothered in more painted foliage — and we walk straight into a glass greenhouse. Long wooden trestle tables skirt the walls, a single one runs straight down the middle. All the tables are covered with pots of various sizes — full-grown plants in some, dustings of green in others, some stand empty. Under the tables are bins of sand, pebbles and peat moss. To our right is a short passageway to a glass door. Through it, I can make out a black table covered with copper bowls, mortars and pestles, jars, crockery pots, knives, wooden spoons and more. Above the table, hanging from wooden rods that crisscross the low ceiling are hundreds of plant bundles.

"My preparation and drying room," Albert says. "At home I have three huge rooms packed full of dried herbs and four large arboretums."

"At home?"

Albert looks flustered. "We — umm — used to live in a much bigger place. Not as, well … bright as here, mind you. We got much more rain. I'm not used to having such limited space, but Poppy said we must fit in here, you know?"

"Fit in? How?"

"Umm … uh … well, this is a pretty closed community. Getting them to rent me a stall space at the market, for instance, was like pulling teeth. I had to show them that we belonged here, so to speak, though *why* I can't really fathom — it's Poppy you see, he gets carried away — puts his *all* into everything …" He looks at me sharply. "Hey, you wouldn't like a job in the mornings, too, would you? Impossible for me to work outside *and* inside right now. I didn't think we'd get noticed here, but … *people* are starting to arrive in droves ever since the market signs went up. Very strange. I've already put feelers out for a couple of other workers and I've only just started! I think it's pointless, really, but Poppy doesn't seem to be in any great hurry to leave and I'd just get bored."

Not understanding what he's burbling about, I say, "I'm not very good at gardening."

"I'd pay the same rate as for Poppy. I'll call your mom if you like."

Rats and double rats! When Mom hears about this, she'll make me take it. But maybe the extra money will allow me to quit sooner and spend most of the holiday with Summer after all.

"Would I have to look after your father in the mornings?" I ask.

"Oh no. He just needs entertaining in the afternoons."

"I guess I could try it for a couple of days — see how it goes. If my parents agree." I can always use them as an excuse to get out of both jobs later on.

"Great!" Albert hugs me and then shrieks, "Yikes! I hope I haven't overcooked my infusion!" He flutters back to the stove.

"What time would you want me in the morning?" I ask, following him.

"Time? Oh yes … time …" He looks at his watch, does some calculating and says, "About nine-ish?"

"Okay. But only if my family doesn't need me —"

He looks at me, puzzled. "How curious. Do you really *care* about your family?"

"Of course I do! I'm the one who watches out for them."

He smiles slowly. "Oh, I'm sure you do, Emma. Yes, of that I'm *sure*."

8

I dump my rain slicker in the basket of my bike and pedal home. I can't believe I'm actually looking forward to coming back here. I really want to play that Fidchell game again. I tried a couple of computer games when Dad had his rented laptop, but Fidchell is a hundred times more fun.

The misty gray sky above is mirrored in the puddles along the road, and the dull atmosphere makes everything hazy and indistinct. By the time I reach Dad's field, my blouse is clinging to my skin. I hear the muffled sound of a saw and spot him on the ladder, his arm vigorously slicing back and forth. He fits right into the circle of hives in the fields around the farm. He's as busy as any of those bees.

I turn onto the farm's pebbled drive, aim the bike at the verandah and, as I pass it, glance through the screened windows. Summer's asleep on the straw lounge, her dark straight hair tumbled around her colorless face. She looks so young and fragile, my heart contracts.

Why can't anyone find out what's wrong with her? When she's well, she's full of zip and energy, but after one of her fall-outs it sometimes takes hours for her to get her strength back. Lately it's taking longer and longer and she seems thinner and more delicate after each attack.

I swallow a hard lump in my throat and walk the bike around the back of the house to once again demand that Mom get her to another doctor. When I peek through the screen door, I can see Mom wrestling with a dead chicken, trying to stuff it with onions and bits of bread. From her scowl, I can tell she's losing the battle. As usual, the kitchen looks like a bomb's gone off in it. I better wait. We'll only end up yelling at each other — something we do a lot of when it comes to Summer.

Dinner is clearly hours away. I know from other kids that most families have a set dinner hour. Not the Sweeneys. Dinner can be anytime between late afternoon and bedtime.

Climbing the barn stairs, I leave the door open so I can sit on my bed and gaze out at the hazy fields. I prop myself on a couple of pillows and soak in the peace, solitude and silence that always act like a spiritual transfusion when I'm tired or worried. The sun comes out for one brief moment, shines through the door and strikes the small piece of amethyst crystal, which instantly shimmers and pulsates as if the sunlight has injected it with life. Curious, I reach over and pick it up.

Suddenly, I am flying into an empty green sky above a boundless ocean, my arms spread out like the wings of a great bird. I lie on the surface of the wind, exhilarated and free. But just as suddenly, the wind dies and I spiral down, down, down.

9

I'm standing in a black space. All the lights in the world have gone out. Stretching my arms in front of me, I shuffle forward, trying to find the light switch. Have I fallen asleep? Is it night? Why didn't anyone call me for dinner? Where's the door? The floor is uneven and crunches underfoot as if I'm walking on stones. Suddenly to my right, a rounded gray shape appears. A doorway?

"Hello? What's happened?" The words form in my mouth but I can't hear them in the thick air that winds around me like a suffocating scarf.

The gray shape floats into a stone archway. I touch the stone's cold roughness, and the muffled silence changes suddenly — into a rushing, watery sound. Reaching one hand out into the dim light, I let my fingers drift through cool water that washes softly over my palm and wrist. A waterfall?

I press wet fingers to my lips. How did I get here? Where *is* here?

Wait … is this a *dream*? It must be. But I never dream. Mom says that vivid dreams show a rich imagination and I think it worries her that I don't dream — like I'm so dull, so boring, that maybe I *can't* dream. Dad just laughs it off, saying lots of people never remember their dreams. Every now and again, Mom asks me if I've had any I can remember, but I always have to say no.

Once she even asked me what kind of *day*dreams I had.

"What's a daydream?" I asked.

She frowned and said, "You know — do you ever imagine yourself in the future? Maybe as a great writer or musician or artist, or ... a doctor? Like do you want to be rich and famous when you grow up?"

"I don't know," I said. "I just go to school, keep an eye on Summer, read ... stuff like that. I don't really know what I want to be. I guess I don't have daydreams."

I think my answer about daydreams upset her more than my not having *night* dreams. Well ... that's what this has to be. A dream. *Amazing.* I almost laugh out loud when I realize I've used Dad's favorite word. Still, the water feels so ... so *real*. I run my hands over my body. I'm still wearing my cotton pants and blouse. Should I try walking through the waterfall? In dreams you can do anything, can't you? But when I stick my hand through the opening, the water stops. Did I accidentally touch a switch in the stone wall?

Putting one foot carefully on the lower lintel of the opening, I stretch forward to peer outside into a green evening light. The thin shells of two moons glow in the sky. The one on my right is orange and hangs in a dark brown sky, while the one on the left is a pale green in a dark green sky, surrounded by a misty halo of blue that wavers as if it's under water. *Two* moons? *Amazing.* That must be allowed in dreams, too.

Just below me, under the green moon, is a beach covered in pale purple sand that stretches to a wide expanse of undulating emerald water. But then, to the right, the sand ends as if someone has sliced a knife right down the middle and replaced half with a shelf of black land and a silhouetted bank of trees. The orange moon sits on the treetops like a giant's eye watching over the wood. It's like I'm seeing two different worlds at once.

Go ahead, go out, a voice inside urges. *It's only a dream. Nothing can happen in a dream.* I inch out through the cave entrance onto a wide ledge. The breeze is warm and smells strongly of the sea, just like the Pacific smelled when my family went there for a vacation a few years ago.

The rock is slippery, but there are easy footholds and my rubber soles keep me from falling. I drop down onto the sand and look around. The forest that was on my right is gone! There's just a long purple strand of beach and beyond that more of the gently rolling sea. Where did the forest go? I run up the rock face. At the cave's entrance, I look back and once again the scene is split as if I'm looking at two different places. The stand of trees is there, dark and brooding. Above it, a rim of clouds moves across the orange moon.

My eyes are drawn back to the ocean side when I see a flicker of something out of the corner of my eye. The dark emerald water is changing color, as if a light is shining up from below. I let out a yelp when a huge glistening creature breaks the surface and surges toward the shore as if it's going to ram it. A long wailing howl echoes through the still air, a tidal wave of sea and foam smacks the shore, and the creature heaves up onto the sand. I hold my breath, but it just lies there, a clear pulsating glob like a giant jellyfish, soggy translucent tendrils trailing behind it. The stench of fish is hot in the air. Can you actually smell things in dreams?

I don't like this dream anymore. I heard somewhere you can pinch yourself awake in a nightmare. I grab some skin and am about to give myself a good pinch when the gooey mass rises up and seems to solidify and glow from within. Dark shadows slide around inside its glassy dome. Then to my horror, with a sound like a deep yawn, the dome cracks open. I back into the cave, pinching myself as hard as I can. Ow. Ow! I run my hands frantically over the cold stone walls. *Wake up, Emma*, the voice inside cries. I can't. I can't! If I can just turn the water back on, maybe I'll be safe. Why won't it turn on? *Wait. Be calm. It's only a dream. Nothing can happen in a dream.*

A shout from below makes my heart stop. In desperation, I shove my hand outside the entrance and like magic the water flows again. Voices come from the beach below. At first I think they're speaking a strange language, but as I listen hard, I hear a faint click inside my head and I can understand them.

"Did you see it, madam?" a man's voice calls. "Up there."

"Where, Huw?" The tinny voice sounds like it's made from an electric synthesizer. I can't tell if it's a man or a woman, but the one called Huw called it "madam," so it must be a woman.

"Where?" a different man calls in a deep, strangled-sounding voice.

"You can make out the entrance behind the water," the one called Huw says. "Quickly, let's go up, madam. With the luck of Ochain, the game can start again!"

The other man cries, "Wait! I want to go, too. Take me!"

"Don't be ridiculous, Keir," the woman says firmly in her weird robot's voice.

The scrape and scatter of stones draws close. I pull back into the darkness with a pounding heart just as shadowy shapes move across the sheet of water outside the cave.

I must stay calm. I can't let them know I'm here. *It's only a dream. Only a dream.* Frantically, I search the darkness for a hiding place.

The one called Keir shouts from below, "We have to find the child, Rhona. We can't give Fergus the lead. I will win my prize. I will *not* lose this game. I won't!"

The woman's strange voice is so close, I can hear the tinny intake of her breath. "I simply cannot convince him to stay calm, can I?" she says quietly. "I hate it when the game grinds to a halt. We can't sit back and wait any longer."

"No, madam, we can't. We've searched and searched the regular portals — none of their keepers has let Fergus pass. That can only mean he's used an old portal. One that hasn't been in play for many eons. This cave holds the fourth of six joint portals along our border. The hounds will tell us if Fergus has used it recently."

"Well? Let's see what's here," Rhona says. Her curious voice rings with authority.

"Stay here, my lady, I beg you. There may be a cunning in there — a trap."

Keir bellows up, "If you'd allowed the Fomor to come with us, they could have carried me up. It's my right!"

"Ach, hold your tongue, Keir," Rhona orders. "Well, Huw? Let's see if we can sniff out Fergus!"

Huw snaps, "Bonda! Tiea! Find!"

I slide into the blackness on the other side of the cave entrance just as two low shapes cut through the water. I back against the stone wall, stare wildly into the gloom, and wish myself invisible. A pair of silvery thick-chested hounds sniff the air, grumble deep in their throats, then surge forward, stopping right in front of me. Four pointed ears are outlined clearly in the grayish light. Jeweled collars glitter on their necks. I almost faint when one of them lets out a loud piercing yelp. The sound echoes deep into the cave. Why don't they attack me?

"Bonda! Tiea!" the man's voice shouts. "Come!"

The hounds turn and spring back through the entrance. I drop to my knees, the muscles in my legs dissolving like pudding.

A human hand carrying a rocket-shaped lantern thrusts through the waterfall, followed by a tall, thin man dressed from neck to toe in tight-fitting leather, one side a dazzling green, the other a speckled, scaly blue. He isn't wearing boots or shoes, for the leathery covering slides right over his feet. His face is a cold, dead white. His pewter gray hair is shaved in a single wide swath from ear to ear, smooth bangs lie flat on his forehead while the back portion has been gathered into a long ponytail covered in a silvery net of pearls. His face is clean shaven except for a wedge-shaped goatee painted with swirls of dull blue. The ear facing me is heavily decorated with more pearls. Black eyes under thick eyebrows scan the space like radar. When he moves, a wave of light like a glowing echo of his shifting figure flutters and sizzles in the air behind him. I rub my eyes, but the blur around him is still there whenever he moves.

I slide on my bottom farther into the inky shadows. He lifts his lantern high and its light glances off my shoe. I pull my foot back and stop breathing, conscious of the empty unguarded air that lies between us, where any sound will give me away. I stay motionless for two or three long minutes. Suddenly he lets out a piercing whistle and the hounds bound into the cave, their nails scrabbling. "Fergus!" he says. "Find." They slide past him toward the darkness at the back of the cave. He follows, leaving behind a trail of echoing light.

Where are they going?

The lamp's glow slides over a wide cavernous hall, highlighting walls decorated in ornate symbols, but I can't make out any details before it disappears around a corner. This man must be Huw. Will the woman called Rhona come through next? Reminding myself that this is my dream and I can do whatever I like in my dream, I creep nervously along behind them. As he moves forward, Huw reaches out now and again, and glass cubes light up one by one.

The cave's walls aren't rough like a real cave, but made up of squares of stone, polished and stacked like a pile of kids blocks, each one the color of old parchment and covered in hieroglyphics of some kind.

Huw turns a corner just ahead and the hounds begin a high-pitched braying. I sneak after them. Huw is standing in the middle of a large room, looking at a small glass table of some kind. From the middle of the table, a purple light, like a thin thread, hangs in the air right up to the cave's ceiling. The hounds run in circles, their noses close to the rough floor. They wuff and growl deep in their throats. Across the space is another cave entrance covered in a net of vines. Some of the trailing creepers have crawled into the cave and wound themselves up around two brown columns at each side of the opening. Will Huw go through it? Will I have the nerve to follow?

He walks along all the walls, searching up and down with his light, while the hounds grow more and more frantic. At one point the angle of his light throws the right side of his face into shadow and illuminates his left cheek, nose and forehead, and I see they're covered in the same swirling patterns painted on his beard, making him look fierce and strangely disfigured.

"Find!" he snarls. "Find!" But the hounds keep running in circles, as if bewildered by the scent they're picking up.

Huw continues his slow examination of the room. To my amazement he walks right past the vine-covered entrance. He stops, backs up and with hands on hips seems to stare in its direction. Then, like a mime, he lays his hands flat against an invisible wall. He pulls back. Waits. Thinks. Knocks on something I can't see and slides his hands in the air, leaving a smear of illumination every few seconds like he's painting the invisible wall in light — but he never moves closer to the cave entrance. I don't think he can see it.

He turns and goes back to the table, points at it and says, "Test. Fix!"

The hounds run to the table and sniff all around it, then begin their horrible braying again, front paws on the table. Huw mutters, "Yes ... he's been here. But why is there no light? A cunning lock! He's put on a cunning lock!" He snarls at the hounds, "Disengage!"

Immediately, they stop howling, sit on their haunches and wait until he snaps out, "Abandon!" They leap past me back the way we came.

Huw remains where he is, staring at the stone table. Why can't he see the purple light? "You won't hide for long, Fergus," he snarls. "I'll break this lock, by Ochain, I'll break it!"

I run back down the hall and try to disappear in a corner of shadow. I'm sure he'll catch me this time, but he walks right past my hiding place to the waterfall. At the mouth of the cave, he halts as if he's been hit with an idea. I hold my breath. His black eyes glint in the light. Can't he see me hovering in the corner? My chest is splitting for breath. When he finally walks quickly through the waterfall, I release my breath with a gasping hiss and run forward to listen.

The woman's electric voice says, "Well? Are we still in the game?"

"The hounds picked up his scent all right. Fergus and his players obviously came in from their own side of the border cave and reopened the hot spot, and as they left, Mathus put a cunning lock on it," Huw says.

"Damnation! But why are we surprised, Huw? Where does this portal go?"

"It's an ancient one. I'll have to consult with the Elder Readers. They have old binnacles that can direct our search. But there's something else in that cave — a presence —"

"What do you mean? An Unseen? A *spy*?"

"No. The hounds would have smelled one of those out in seconds."

"The point is, Huw, this means the game begins again!" she says loudly, excitement making her robot's voice shrill and high.

"Please, my queen. We don't want Keir hearing this."

She whispers fiercely, "We must make plans, Huw. Fergus could be in one of a dozen worlds! Some are very dangerous. We'll have to be prepared for anything."

"And we'll have to move fast," he replies. "If we admit to Keir that Fergus's group was here, he'll tell anyone and everyone that the game is on again — an Unseen could immediately send a warning to Fergus, who will move on. We don't want to start the search all over again."

"Why don't we get one of the Hidden Tribe — a Watcher — to go ahead of us to search out Fergus?" the woman says. "Watchers can slide from world to world without portals."

"Even most Watchers can't go through a strong cunning lock, my queen. And there's such a lock on this gate — one I don't recognize. This will be Mathus's doing. When I crack the puzzle we'll find out which world Fergus and he have entered. But remember, most of the old realms have removed their return gates, so they must be rebuilt from the other side. We can't risk going through this one without knowing we can return at will — and quickly."

Rhona's voice is low and intense. "I'll take your guidance on this, Huw. Mathus is a powerful Druvid. Let us hope you can free his cunning lock. Come. It's late. I have much to think about."

I hear the strength and certainty in her weird voice and know that she's definitely the one in control.

Huw says urgently, "We must keep this from your brother. We don't want Keir doing anything that will jeopardize our strategy."

"I give you my word, Huw, that —"

"Well?" Keir shouts from below.

Why didn't he come up to the waterfall with the other two?

"Is it the place?" he demands. "Tell me! Am I right?"

"Stop that bellowing!" the woman calls back.

I hear the crunch of stones. Thank god, they're leaving. I'm about to stand up when the dogs slide back through the waterfall and lurk inside the cave entrance like menacing sentinels.

"You see, madam?" Huw says. "The hounds feel the strange presence as well. Fergus may have his Watcher Tamhas keeping a close eye on the portal. Bonda! Tiea! Come."

They whirl back through the water. I lean against the stone wall to slow my heart. That's when it dawns on me that neither the man nor the dogs were wet when they came into the cave, despite passing through drenching water.

The crunch of stones fades. I know they must be walking across the sand toward Keir and that strange vessel-creature thing that waits below.

The silent wash of the waterfall is the only sound in the cave for a long time. Who are these people? Who's the one they call Fergus? Why didn't either the dogs or Huw see me? Why didn't Huw see the opening at the far end of the cave? Will I ever wake up again?

10

Sitting here isn't going to wake me up. Pinching doesn't work. Maybe the way back home is through the room with the purple light. Using the walls and my memory as guides, I slowly inch my way down the black hallway. Finally, just when I start getting panicky, I see the thread of light and the vague gray archway of the other cave entrance.

I walk carefully past the light toward the vine-covered opening. When I push aside the heavy creepers, the orange moon winks out from behind some clouds and bathes everything in a sickly light. I'm high on a cliff above the forest — the huge leaves of palmlike trees and thick bundled foliage spread out like a lumpy carpet far, far below. To my left I can see what looks like a path — but how can that be? As my eyes adjust to the light, I realize that what I'm seeing is some sort of bridge made out of closely woven vines. If a person falls in a dream, does she wake up? Can she die? I've never been afraid of heights, but this is way higher than a tall building, and that bridge looks pretty spindly.

Sucking in a deep breath, I cross a narrow ledge to the woven pathway. The railings are loops of vines, the uppermost support as thick as my arm and covered in a rough peeling bark. One step at a time, I edge forward, ready to spring back into the cave if I have to. I'm too scared to look down, but I look left to see if I can make out the ocean. It's nowhere in sight. There's just the stretch of high cliff and more jungly forest. Why can't I see the water? And when I was on the sand, why couldn't I see the jungle? It's almost as if the two worlds stand side by side but separate — except through the cave. Huw called it a border cave. But the border between what?

The bridge path lies straight ahead for about ten paces, but then it seems to curve in mid-air down toward the interior of the forest. What should I do? Explore or turn back and figure out a way to wake up? I bite my bottom lip and keep going. The woven grasses and vines hold my weight. I walk gingerly along their narrow width, gripping tightly onto the railing.

I'm so busy keeping my balance that the first shaft of lightning and splat of heavy raindrops shock me. A blast of howling wind sheers across me, tearing at my clothes. The bridge starts to sway. I turn to run back to the cave but twist and fall to one side, clinging frantically to a railing slick with wet.

What tripped me? Why can't I move my foot? Dashing away my streaming bangs, I watch in horror as a thin tendril from the lower railing winds itself around my ankle, tighter and tighter. The whole bridge breathes and expands in the rain — monster leaves unfold with wet rushing sounds, while red spears of new growth stream out into the air and then slide back into the foliage like snakes. In seconds, the whole bridge is a heaving tangled mass of vegetation rising up around me.

I grab the binder around my leg and pull, but it only straps itself tighter. I frantically unwind it, all the while trying to keep my balance as the bridge sways and dips. Round and round my hands go, and suddenly, miraculously I'm free. I run toward the cave, slashing aside vegetation that appears out of nowhere. I sob with relief when I see the entrance to the cave just ahead. But a wall of foliage instantly whips around in front of me — so tangled and dense there's no way I'll ever get through it.

This is a dream! This is a dream! The voice inside my head cries out. *You can do anything in a dream! Anything!*

I close my eyes and jump forward and suddenly I'm flying up through the air. I aim at the cave's entrance, spin through the vines and hit the floor with a thud. I sit up and rub my shoulder. Lightning slashes and rain thunders down outside. Vines clatter into the cave, leaves bursting out, tendrils uncoiling like pythons ready to squeeze the life out of me. I could run out the other opening to the sea, but then what? I have to go home. I have to wake up.

Huw said this cave was a portal. A portal is a door, isn't it? I scramble toward the purple light, crouch down and fearfully, but with a certainty I have to do it, reach out and touch the light with my fingertip. A numbing electric current jolts into my arm, and with a sickening lurch I fly straight up through the roof of the cave.

When I wake, my whole body is trembling. It takes me a second or two to realize that Summer is shaking me.

"I know, I know," she says, when I push her hand away. "I'm not supposed to enter your *domain*, but Mom is holding dinner for you. She's made you a yucky chickpea curry."

I stare at her. My hand throbs painfully, like it's been stung by a bee.

"What's with you? Get up. Hey! Where've you been? You're all dirty and wet! Yuck!" She looks worried. "Are you okay, Emmy?"

My clothes are soaked, the knees of my cream-colored pants black with dirt, my carefully polished shoes scuffed and scraped. I open my aching hand. The crystal rolls onto the bedcover. The tip of my right index finger has a blister forming on the exact spot where I touched that amethyst-colored light.

11

I eat a few mouthfuls of curry and feel sick. Even half an hour later, dressed in dry, clean clothes, I still feel disoriented and confused by my dream. And to make things worse, Dad's just announced he's hired Tom Krift to work a few hours every day in his field.

"Jeez, Dad, I could have worked for you," I say, "instead of having to go to those weird Maxims."

"I'm sorry, Emma. I knew you'd taken on the job with them — at fifteen bucks an hour. The kid's going to clear brush from my site, that's all. And I'm paying him half what you're getting. He just happened to come by — so I asked him."

I try to swallow my anger with a mouthful of curry but it almost chokes me. He didn't even think to ask me.

"You okay, Wint— Emma?" Mom asks. She's passing by with a plate of fruit and puts it on the table to feel my forehead. "You're hot."

I pull away and mumble, "Yeah, well … it's like an oven in here."

"Hey, Emmy, maybe you're allergic to work!" Summer says. "I hope I am, too. I'm allergic to everything else." She pours thick gravy over her chicken and then stares at it. She's always staring at her food instead of eating it.

"Well, Ms. Spock," Dad says to me, dipping a chunk of banana into a small bowl of honey and shoveling it, dripping, into his mouth. "How *was* your first day of work? Nice people?"

I shrug, still irritated. Calling me Spock is another of Dad's little jokes. He thinks I'm like Mr. Spock on *Star Trek* — too logical, too dull. Like Mom, he really means I have no imagination. Too bad they weren't in that weird dream with me. That'd soon change their minds.

He says, "By the way, thanks for keeping the amethyst for me. I'll take it back to the site in a day or so." He points at the plastic bag I dropped on the counter when I walked in.

I don't want to talk about his chunk of purple rock. The broken bit is hidden in my pocket. To divert him, I say, "Albert Maxim asked me to work in his greenhouse for a few hours in the mornings, but I said I wasn't sure —"

"That's great!" Mom exclaims. "It would help *so much*, Emma."

Apparently my feelings don't count.

Summer says, "Emmy was having some sort of nightmare when I went to get her for dinner, weren't you, Emmy? I had to shake her real hard, and her face was all scared and crazy looking when she woke up."

"That's what you get for napping before dinner," Mom says. "My dad always said that daytime dreams were much more potent than night dreams. They can be portents — messages of things to come. Did you dream, Emma? What was it about?"

I say curtly, "I don't remember."

"I was napping, too," Summer says importantly. "And *I* had the *weirdest* dream. I was walking through a dark jungle and someone was following me. It was really creepy." She shivers dramatically.

"I looked at you through the screen when I got home," I offer. "That's why you thought you were being watched — because you were." Still, it's odd how much her dream and mine are alike. Is that how dreams work — do family members sometimes dream similar things?

I ask, "Were there any people in your dream other than the one you couldn't see — the one following you?"

Summer looks surprised. "I don't know. Why?"

I push my chair back. "No reason, I think I'll go for a walk."

"Great idea," Dad says. "You can take this to Tom." He lifts up a duffel bag with a pair of long-handled pruning shears sticking out of it.

I snap, "Can't you take it to him tomorrow?"

"No, he said he'd work for a while this evening. Take Summer with you. She could do with some fresh air. Just go slow."

Summer's eyes widen. "Not me! Lacey's coming over." She flicks her hair behind her ears. "She bought this little bag of different nail colors, like orange, lime, purple and stuff, and we're going to do each nail a different color. Fingers *and* toes."

Dad holds the bag up. "It won't take more than fifteen minutes, Emma, and it'll blow the cobwebs out. You look pretty saggy from your sleep."

"Better wear duck boots," Mom says. "It'll be messy walking."

"Tell him not to burn that brush," Dad adds. "I'll do it tomorrow. I have a permit. He doesn't."

He flicks on the CD player hiding under a pile of newspapers and they begin the dishes, gyrating to blaring rock music. Dad does a shuffle-hop, Mom sways and Summer prances like a scrawny little pony, her thin face glowing. Dishes clatter and water splashes. Dad puts his arms around Mom and off they go tango-ing across the room. Mom's face is flushed and she's laughing like a kid.

Sometimes it makes me really angry that Dad seems to get away with hanging out in a field building a giant play gym while Mom works long hard hours to keep money coming in. Before we moved here, she used to do people's taxes and lots of accounting for small businesses from our apartment. Sometimes I'd get up in the middle of the night to get a glass of water and find her still working, books and papers piled around her while my father snored happily. Since we moved here, she's working harder than ever. Sometimes I can't figure out why she doesn't just lose it and tell him to find a real job. But then seeing them like this, his face plastered with a goofy smile, I know they've somehow worked it all out and they'll always be nuts about each other. And I feel left out.

Fighting down that familiar wave of sadness, I leave them to it and plod across the road, my rubbered feet slapping the cracked blacktop, the heavy bag dragging on my shoulder. The evening sun has pushed its way through the gray mist. My fresh clothes are already sticking to me. The sun steams the wetness into a thin vapor that trails through the ditches and up from the puddles on the road. To my relief, inside the grove of trees it's a bit cooler. The slanting light scatters yellow cutouts across the ground.

I'm not exactly thinking about the events of the day — just letting the patterns of my mind slide over and around them randomly like those sunspots on the path, trying not to examine the sad feelings that drift in and out — when suddenly my mind goes very still. A shadow is moving alongside me on the other side of the bushes. I stare straight ahead, letting my peripheral vision take in everything, my ears straining to hear every sound.

A faint snap and then the soft thud of a footfall sounds to my left. I swing my head slowly, scanning foliage that seems suddenly closer and more sharply focused. One section of hazelnut bush that was solid now has sun filtering through it. Someone was hiding there and has moved on.

It could have been a deer, but I know it wasn't. The faint odor of human sweat mixed with a hint of cloves floats to me on a puff of breeze. I hitch the duffel bag higher and trot quickly through the trees.

When I reach Dad's work site, Tom Krift is nowhere in sight, but a white T-shirt lies on the ground by the tent.

"Hello?" I call.

"Over here!" a voice shouts from the riverbank.

Was Tom Krift spying on me in the woods? I lower the duffel bag to the ground and backtrack a bit. Behind the tent, the Brokenhead runs alongside a frothing line of willows. Here the river is shallow, its sandy bottom barely ankle deep in spots. Tussocks of grass and sandy patches stand above the waterline.

Tom Krift sits on one of the small grassy hills, his feet in the gently moving current. He's bare-chested, his pants are rolled up to his knees and he's staring at something with great concentration.

His body is wide and pale and muscular. In the golden light, his homely face is so filled with humor I hardly recognize him. He turns his head and looks up at my flushed face. The leather strap around his neck has a strange silver disk with a moon symbol attached to it.

"Were you just walking around over there?" I gesture toward the stand of trees.

"Me? No. I've been sitting right here for ages. Why?"

"I — uh — I brought you a pair of long-handled shears," I say, quickly. "I left them by the tent."

Something moves in the willows behind him. I hold my breath and stare at the trembling leaves. A yellowthroat warbler flutters out and streaks across to another bush, searching and clicking. I start breathing again. My dream and the shadowy figure in the woods have unnerved me.

Tom points at something across the narrow channel. "I've been watching that mother duck and her three babies. See the one with the tuft on his head? He's a risk taker. He paddles farther away all the time, until his mama panics and calls him back. Then she scolds him, but as soon as her back is turned, he's off again. And that one with the single feather sticking straight up on her wing ... well, she's spent the whole time trying to get the other little ducks in line. She's stubborn and determined. But she's too focused on controlling what they're doing, and my worry is that she'll be so distracted that she won't see danger before it's on her."

I've never heard Tom talk this much. At school he was definitely a "yup" or "nope" guy. He continues. "Now, that tiny one over there ... he's not very bright, but he's having a lot of fun. He's the smallest and weakest, but he'll survive out of sheer dumb luck."

The smallest duck's little bottom is in the air while he searches for food. He tips upright again and shakes himself exuberantly.

"Reminds me of my little sister," I say.

Tom looks at me. "And you? Are you like one of them?"

"Me? Absolutely not!"

He grins. "Are you sure? Well, I suspect I'm the one who keeps wandering off. Getting into trouble."

He leans forward and tosses a handful of crumbs at the little ducks. In the warm light, the flat muscles slide loosely under his skin. I take a few steps back, barely feeling my feet, before I turn and start up the riverbank. I hear water splash and soon he's walking beside me carrying his work boots.

When we get to Dad's tent, I show him the shears.

"They'll do," he says, pushing his arms into his T-shirt and pulling it over his head.

"Okay. I'll — well, I'll see you," I murmur, turning to go.

"This thing your Dad's building. Do you know what it is?" he asks casually, but his eyes never leave my face.

I shrug. "It's a plastic circle henge. He's always doing something bizarre. He'll finish this, and a bunch of arty types will come and ooh and aah, and photographers will record it — and soon after he'll move on to something else, like a giant ice-cream cone made out of rusty lunch boxes."

He laughs. "He has no idea what he's really doing then?"

"What do you mean?"

It's Tom's turn to shrug. "You're not too happy that I'll be working for your dad on and off."

"Doesn't matter to me what you do."

"You've gotten even skinnier than you were at school. Are you all right?"

"What business is that of yours?"

"Oops. Sorry. *None* of my business, I guess. I know you like privacy — that's why you hide out on the farm."

"I do *not* hide out."

He says, "You hardly ever smile. Are you so serious and sad all the time? You have a nice smile. It's a shame you don't use it more often."

I snap. "For someone who said all of two words in class, you suddenly have a whole lot to say that's *none of your business*."

He bows. "I beg your pardon. Forgive me, my lady."

I know he's teasing me, and I say coldly, "I've got to get back home. My father says please don't light any fires. It's against the law."

I keep walking, but I think I hear him say, "Aaah, but you have no laws, little Creirwy, if only you but knew it."

12

Naturally, I catch my shorts on the fence. With great dignity, I unhitch them and lower myself to the ground. When I get back to the farm, Mom's watering a row of straggly petunias in front of the verandah.

"They're all in the kitchen making chocolate ice cream," she calls. "You want some?"

I shake my head and aim toward the barn.

"Emma? Come here a minute."

Reluctantly I go. I've had enough of everything for one day. I don't want to talk.

She rests both hands on my shoulders. "You're such a little loner, aren't you? Everything okay?"

"You ask me that all the time. Nothing's ever quite okay, is it?"

"You know," she says, searching my face, "when I was near your age, my mom said that I was about to enter what she called The Borderland — a territory between childhood and adulthood. It's a scary place, she said — a vast world of change, some good, some not so good — and she wanted me to be ready for it. Growing up isn't easy, Emma."

"Do you *like* being a grown-up?"

She smiles. "It took me a long time to figure out what I truly wanted. But yeah — it's got its good points."

"I guess I'm like you were once," I say. "I don't have any idea what I'm supposed to do with my life. You're a beekeeper now, like your dad. Maybe I'll stay here and become a beekeeper, too."

She gives me a funny look. "Only if you choose to, sweetheart. I never thought I'd become a beekeeper. I saw how isolated my parents were — like everyone else in this town. Your Grandma Rose came from Limestone — a fifteen minute drive away — where other Scots settled. You know, she hardly ever saw her parents after she married."

"You said once that outsiders only come to Bruide by marrying someone from town," I say.

"Yes, that's right."

"Like Dad?"

She blinks at me, then laughs. "Yeah, in a weird sort of way, I guess that's right. Anyway, I don't think my mother and father ever traveled much farther than Limestone in their whole lives. And of course your grandpa expected me to stay here for the rest of my life — to take over when he got too old. I wanted to get away — to experience life, you know? But he kept telling me there was more to see and experience right here on the farm than I would ever find away. That's what he called it. Away."

"But you went ... away — to university."

"I did. Mom used some money she inherited and sent me to Winnipeg. My father was angry about it for years. After she died, he guilted me into coming home now and again. But I had no intention of returning for good."

"So, why have you come back then?"

She shrugs. "I guess I'm a farm girl at heart after all. Oh, I tried — I even thought the city was exciting at first, but ... well, it was all game playing and one-upmanship. Who could beat the other guy to the best job, the best lifestyle, even the best parking stall. One day, I was standing on the forty-fourth floor, looking down at the traffic and listening to the phones ring all around me, and I said to myself, 'I *hate* this.' None of it was *real*, you know? I'd just known your dad a few weeks but I think he'd already changed the way I looked at things. He did his own thing. But he also accepted me for who I was. In all the years we've been together, he's never tried to change me to become someone I'm not."

"But you still worked doing other people's accounts and taxes — wasn't that part of the world you hated so much?"

"People have to work, honey. But with a home office, I could still be with my girls. Life's always a compromise." She ruffles my hair. "I want you to be able to survive out there. I think we've kept you too isolated. That's why I keep harping at you to go to university — then you can make up your mind which road you'll take —"

I tried to smile reassuringly. "I'll be okay. Really."

She nods, eyeing me uncertainly. "And this work at the Maxims'? I didn't force you … too hard?"

"No — it's okay."

I can tell she's relieved that our conversation is over. "Good." She kisses my cheek. "Off to bed?"

I nod. Summer's voice, followed by a shriek from Lacey, floats out the side window. "Daddy! Raspberry, not *peach* syrup! You can't put peach syrup on chocolate ice cream! Uck!"

I walk up the steps to the loft, put on my cotton pajamas, reach for a new book and sit down on my window seat. Mom's gone back into the house and I can hear them all laughing. Why does their laughter make me feel like crying? It's like everything is piling up inside me — having to work for those weird Maxims, Mom's pressure to go to university, Summer getting sick more and more often. That last worry stops my heart. Is that why I'm so sure that my family's time together is getting shorter and shorter? I can't *know* that Summer's going to die. The doctors have assured Mom that Summer will outgrow these allergies or whatever they are. I *have* to trust them. I especially have to trust Mom and Dad. My stomach winds into a tighter knot.

What if all these so-called grown-ups are wrong?

I can't think like this anymore. I'll just keep a closer eye on Summer, and if she starts getting worse, I'll ... what *will* I do? I feel so helpless. So *useless*. It's more than just Summer. Something tells me that my whole family is heading toward something bad. Which is crazy. I mean, Summer *is* actually sick. But there's no sign of anything else wrong — Mom and Dad are fine. I have to get hold of myself. *I have to.*

I stare out the window, searching for comfort in the lowering sun that melts like warm marmalade into the driveway puddles. In the distance the wind-break of willows and the small knot of trees in the center of the far bee field are hazy and indistinct. Sometimes when evening falls like this, the sight of the open fields fills me with a strange kind of ... homesickness — a longing for a place where I can grow and change and become the somebody I know is hidden deep inside me. Someone light and free. Whoever *she* is.

Across the yard, the back screen door slaps shut and Dad's truck drives out from behind the house — heading for town, driving Lacey home. In a few minutes it returns. Then another slap of the screen door, and soon all the lights in the house go off. The yard light flicks on and, a few minutes later, off. It won't go on again unless someone walks close to the house.

I can't help Summer by watching over the silent house. Besides, she had a pretty good day despite the fall-out and she actually recovered her energy quite fast this time. I shift over to my straw bed and stare at the darkening ceiling above, letting my mind drift everywhere except to my family. I don't know why this feeling of being on guard has grown suddenly so intense, but it makes me restless and uneasy.

Slowly, images from the day churn through my head: Albert's freckled face and big ears; the old man's toothy grin looming like a monstrous jack-o'-lantern's; the excitement of the Fidchell game; Tom and the woman on horseback; the scent of cloves, of the sea, of damp earth; silver dogs leaping through glittering water; a man with strange hair and a tattooed face; and vines that want to drag me into a frightening black jungle.

If I sleep, will I go back into that dream world? I've always thought I faced things head-on. But how can you face something that isn't even *real* — that comes from inside yourself?

I force my eyes shut, but my body remains as stiff as the planks around my bed. I try to listen for the night sounds that normally lull me to sleep —

like the call of the large white barn owl as it slides in and out of the hayloft. It arrived a few weeks ago and its strange straw-sipping cry unnerved me until I discovered what it was. Sometimes I like to sit on the wide beam on the other side of the trap door and wait for it to return from the hunt. I always feel happy when I see its gentle heart-shaped face floating through the barn's rafters, wishing that I could fly, too. But tonight I hear only the distant chirrup of crickets and the chee chee of tiny frogs in the ditches along the road.

I grow more and more restless. Finally, I glance at the window seat that faces the house. I'm not going to sit there all night. I'm *not*. Instead, I climb through the trap door in the side wall and crawl onto the massive beam. The owl's regular perch is empty. I'm wide awake now. I'll wait.

I've just settled cross-legged on the beam when I hear a scurrying sound on the barn floor. Mom and Dad use the barn mainly for storage — randomly scattered boxes and other junk crowd the wide space. Must be a mouse. There it is again — a swish and a scuttle, followed by a loud thump, as if something has fallen off one of the boxes. Alarm, like prickly footed insects, crawls up my legs when the side door below creaks open. I lean forward and peer into the darkness. The black silhouette of a man stands outlined in the open doorway. He slides outside and the door snaps shut.

I crawl back into my room and run to the window facing the house. A figure is running across the yard. When the outside light suddenly flashes on, the figure veers to one side and heads for the road, but not before I see who it is.

What the heck is Tom Krift doing skulking in my barn?

I'm down the stairs in two seconds, running flat out. He'll have to travel across the open expanse of yard to get to the road. But when I reach the end of our driveway there's no one in sight. The highway is silent, no sound of an engine — not even the clop of horse's hooves. I stand, hands on hips, gasping for air. Did he follow me home? Why? I turn and limp back across the yard. I didn't notice the sharp gravel when I was running. Now it stings the soles of my feet. As I climb the stairs, the large pale owl flies gently over my head and swoops into the barn. I hope his hunt was more successful than mine.

13

The next morning the sun is a yellow explosion in the early sky. A meadowlark trills up and down the scale and bees float like tiny airships above the clover.

Mom is making honey cakes. Half the table is covered with her debris, the other half occupied by Summer's mess. She's putting labels onto plain glass and honey-bear bottles with squeeze caps.

"Off to work?" Mom stirs the batter with a whap whap of the spatula.

"Will Summer be with you all day?" I ask.

"Jeeez, Emmy, I'm not a baby. Mom and I are busy. Go away!"

"Summer, that's enough," Mom says. "And as for you, Emma, my love, I *think* I can look after one of my own daughters without the other one hovering like an overprotective grandmother. You are becoming more and more like your new name."

Miffed, I decide not to tell her about the visitor to the barn last night. Maybe later, when I feel less irritated by the two of them happily messing around in the kitchen.

I pedal past Dad's henge field. He's high on a ladder hammering away. Should I talk to him about Tom? I call and wave, but he doesn't hear me. I pedal faster, even more irritated.

Just to add its two cents worth, my bike starts to clatter. Then it begins to wobble. I have no tools with me and if I go back home I'll be late. I grind my way along the road, puffing and snarling and covered in sweat.

A couple of cars drive past me on the dirt road to the Maxims', their windows crowded with plants. When a squat minivan forces me onto the rutted shoulder, I give up in fuming disgust and push the clattering bike up to the house, where Albert Maxim is loading his truck with gardening tools. He's wearing duck boots, his enormous straw hat, dark sunglasses, paint-spattered shorts and a dark cotton shirt.

"Hiya!" he cries. "Right on time. But then I knew you would be. You're that sort of person, aren't you? Reliable."

I lean the bike against the house, tuck my shirt in, pull my belt tighter. Yes, I am reliable. And steady. And in control.

"Can I borrow a wrench?" I ask.

"No probleemo," he trills. "In the truck."

I find a small wrench in an old toolbox behind the seats and I'm able to tighten the chain a bit. With luck it'll hold on the way home.

"All set?" Albert calls, climbing into the driver's side of the truck.

"Are we going somewhere? Aren't I supposed to work in the greenhouse?"

"Oh, no. I need you in the fields today."

I hop into the other seat and throw the wrench back into the toolbox. Albert giggles. "You've got grease on your forehead." While I rub at it, he continues, "I thought we'd do the basil patch first — it's over in the sunniest part of the field. Then we'll work our way through the rosemary and on to the lavender and Saint John's wort."

"Saint John's *wart*?"

"Actually, we call it felon, but people here call it Saint John's wort — with an *O* not an *A*. In the lore of your past world, this man, Saint John, wore a belt of it in the wilderness and survived all sorts of dire things." He starts the truck and heads down the road. "From that time on, people thought it would keep the wanderer safe from fatigue, sunstroke, wild beasts and evil spirits. I make it into an infusion for nerves and salts for the bath. Very relaxing. I hope to sell lots of it. Everyone is so stressed in this world, aren't they? I mean even in this small town they're unbelievably stressed. I gave some felon drops to the fellow who *finally* gave me a market stall. Name of

MacIvor. He didn't want to let me in, but I managed to convince him. Seemed quite rattled after our negotiations." He looks at me with a smirk and rubs the fingertips of one hand together. "Money always talks, eh? Even here. So ... let's go, Emma. More money to make, eh? Though what good it will do us in the *end*, I have no idea."

"What if people come to buy something later on? There's no one at the house," I point out.

"Oh, but I *have* someone," he says happily. "I briefed her this morning and gave her a list of prices. She knows the plants, and I think she'll work out fine. Mind you, it's all a waste of time in my opinion ..." He glances slyly at me, then shrugs and concentrates on the road.

The sun wavers behind a wall of trembling heat. I half close my eyes against the searing light glancing off the truck's hood, so I don't really take in what I'm seeing until we're practically on top of it.

"Aaah, there's my other new helper," Albert trills.

Tom Krift, in shorts, T-shirt and ball cap. He's hoeing a long row of purple plants.

"He's your new worker?" I ask accusingly. "You said it was a woman!"

"No, the woman is working at the greenhouse. This is my new field hand, Tom Krift. I understand I'm sharing him with your father."

He waves at Tom Krift, who frowns at me — as if somehow I've intruded on *his* life. Talk about nerve.

Albert asks, "Do you know him?"

"Barely," I mutter.

"Well, he's made a big dent in the weeds in the purple basil, so why don't we start on the rosemary patch?"

The rosemary field is right beside the purple basil. I turn my back on Tom Krift and begin to scrape furiously with a hoe, all the while trying to think of a way to get him to confess what he was doing hanging around my barn. After a while the hard work distracts me from my angry thoughts. I'm surprised at how huge the herb patches are and how vigorously weeds have sprung up everywhere. I was woolly headed and tired when I started, and it's much worse now. If Albert had called and warned me, I would've worn boots and socks. My sandals are caked in dirt, and by the time we reach the lavender beds, I'm soaked in sweat and my back and legs ache horribly.

Finally Albert calls, "Break time."

I drop my hoe in the dirt. Blisters have popped up all over my palms, the finger with the burn on it is bleeding where the skin sloughed off, and there's a weird thumping beat at the back of my head. I am not happy.

"Hey, I thought you only worked at your own farm," Tom Krift says, appearing at my side with a plastic glass of lemonade.

"Really? And what business is that of yours?" The sunlight makes my eyes burn.

"None, as usual," he says, grinning. "You didn't mention working for Albert, that's all. Hey, this sun is lethal and you aren't wearing a hat. You feeling all right?"

I glower at him. How can he talk to me in such a normal voice when he was lurking around my barn last night? I open my mouth to attack, but Albert interrupts.

"You're right, Tom. I should have insisted she wear a hat."

"I'm fine," I snarl, even though my head has a rubber mallet thumping on it.

Both gaze at me for a moment, then Albert tosses his drink out of the glass and says, "Come on. I don't like that glazed look. I should have remembered who you are. You can't take the sun any more than I can."

I try to argue, but my tongue has turned into a dusty rag in my mouth. Albert clucks like a worried hen and hustles me toward the truck. I turn and glare at Tom Krift, "I want to talk to you!" I shout, but it comes out, "Aagwantatagayoog!" I consider trying again, but my head hurts too much.

Albert pushes me into the passenger's seat. On the way down the road, which has suddenly developed far too many bumps for my liking, he asks, "What was that all about?"

"Nuffig," I moan, swallowing hard to keep from throwing up. I lean my pounding head back on the seat and will myself to stay in control.

When we arrive at the stone farmhouse, Albert marches me into the kitchen, puts a cold cloth on the back of my neck, opens a cupboard and, after some consideration, selects a small bottle and offers me a spoonful of syrup from it.

The monster vegetables on the wall swirl around me, looking like stewed spinach. Yuck. I close my eyes and shake my head.

"Smells awful. Throw up," I say, but it, too, comes out all garbled. I try whispering it and that works.

Albert laughs. "You won't throw up. It'll take away the nausea, and maybe help the headache."

I shake my head again, then hold it with both hands. "I'm ... I think my head is going to burst," I whisper.

He reaches forward and pinches my nose hard. Shocked, I open my mouth to catch a breath and he tosses the spoonful of liquid into it.

"Uck! What are you doing —" I begin, but stop. The nausea has eased almost instantly.

"Better?" he asks, handing me a fresh cold cloth.

"Head still hurts," I whisper, tears prickling my eyes.

A woman strides into the kitchen, catches sight of me and smiles, as if she knows a big secret and is keeping it to herself. It's the woman I saw on horseback yesterday with Tom Krift. Something deep inside me slides away and hides.

"Well, *she* doesn't look very good. Is this the Sweeney who looks after your papa?" she asks Albert.

"Yes," Albert says. "This is *she*. Emma, this is Janet Krift. Tom's mother."

The woman is stocky and dark like her son, with the same straight black eyebrows. Her hair is tied back with a strip of brown cotton. She wears a pair of tight brown cords and a green shirt tucked into a surprisingly small waist. Her hands are large and strong and without jewelry, her face long and sharp-edged, her eyes a strange urgent yellow that reminds me of a grackle staring down from a tree branch.

Albert says, "I needed Emma in the field. That sun is just too hot. I hate it. It sears my eyes! Now she's not feeling well."

The woman moves swiftly toward me, takes my hand and examines it, running her fingers over the birthmark. "*Two* moons, eh? With an arrow shaft through them. Interesting."

Her comment shakes me a bit. I'd never thought the birthmark looked like much of anything until Dad said he thought it looked like two blurry crescent moons with a tiny arrow joining them. Odd that she'd think the same thing. She lifts my chin in her hand. I stare into yellow eyes that see inside my head.

"Mmm, yes. She has no idea of course —," the woman says matter-of-factly. "But even so, she'll not stay here with you long. She'll *have* to go back. It's the child. It's her nature. Inbred. You can only distract her for so long, you see."

"Huh?" is all I can say.

Albert says quickly, "Nothing to worry about, Janet. The girl is feeling terribly ill. Sunstricken?" He looks at Janet appealingly. "You know I have little experience with the sun."

"But where are you from then?" I mutter.

Janet says, "British Columbia. He's exaggerating."

Once again, she leans over me. I slide back in my chair to avoid her, but this time she doesn't touch me. She moves her hands in the air around my head, shakes them as if they're wet and circles them around my head again. Standing back, she shakes them a final time and says, "Better?"

To my amazement, I *am* better. My headache has almost gone.

She smiles a lofty smile and says to Albert, "Let her take a light lunch into the front room. A little rest will help. If she continues to feel better, she can carry on with her work." She leans one hip against the counter, her eyes never leaving my face. "Odd isn't it — we need her and yet we *don't.*"

Albert says loudly, as if trying to drown out her words, "Janet is starting her own business — healing therapy."

Janet shrugs casually. "Eons ago, I traveled all over this curious world at various times. The Folk had quite a lot of knowledge — a small number of them still do. However, they lack the art of balancing internal stresses with meridian energy —"

"How about some lunch?" Albert interrupts, his voice high. "Then, if you still feel ill, Emma, I'll take you home. Poppy can amuse himself for one afternoon."

Janet, that secret smile never leaving her face, pushes away from the counter and walks through the door into the greenhouse, closing it behind her. Good riddance.

Albert looks as relieved as I feel. I watch him tear up three different types of lettuce leaves. He slices cucumbers, white and purple radishes and finally a huge red tomato. He makes a dressing of buttermilk, garlic and handfuls of herbs, before slicing some sort of brown seed bread.

He puts a little salad on a small plate, sets it aside and prepares a large tray for the old man.

"Even if you can't stay, I hope you will take him his meal later," he says. "I'd like you to pour him some iced tea as well. It's in the fridge."

I nod silently, take the small plate of salad he offers me and follow the vines to the "front" room. No wonder I had dreams about vines crawling all over me. These look so real I half expect them to wind around me and drag me back to my nightmare. The room has a brown couch, a darkly patterned rug and some big pillows scattered across the floor. The walls are splashed with what look like pre-historic water lilies, arrowhead flowers and strange pale-eyed fish floating through a deep grayish green wash. I find the artwork ugly and frightening. Not at all like the blue-green ocean in my dream. But, a little voice says, that thing that came out of the ocean wasn't exactly from Disneyland, was it?

I sit on the couch and pick at the salad. Something is nagging at me. I think and think, and suddenly it's as if someone lifts the top of my head and drops in a single word.

Child.

The old man upstairs mentioned a child. Now this Janet person. Even the people in my dream talked about a child. And each time the word is mentioned, it's as if the speaker has put a small intense spotlight on it.

I can hear the one called Keir from my dream, his voice as clear as if he's standing right beside me.

"We have to find the child, Rhona. We can't give Fergus the lead. I will win my prize. I will not lose this game. I won't!"

Why is everyone talking about a child? Can it be the *same* child? No ... that's silly. One of those people comes from my dream. And he isn't even *real*.

I pull the five-sided piece of amethyst out of my pocket and hold it. Was it somehow responsible for my dream yesterday? It grows icy cold in my hand, the watery walls shift closer. I feel my body lift off the couch. I float for a second or two, then take a big gulp of air and swim straight up through cold dark green water. Inky shadows flash past me in the murky depths. Fear makes me kick harder and soon the water changes, growing warmer, turning a translucent emerald. I can see rock formations nearby with a large shadowy crevice just ahead. Suddenly, a monstrous shape surges straight up at me through the green water, bubbles streaming around it. The surface is too far away. Terrified, I give a great thrust with my legs and slide into the crevice. Something bangs against the rocks with a deep muffled roar. I can't go back out there. I feel the tug of a current and behind me I see a distant light. I kick my feet and swim toward it. I can't hold my breath any longer. My lungs are bursting. Lights shatter in my head and everything goes black.

14

I'm lying on a damp leaf-strewn floor in a small room, not much bigger than a closet. There are no windows, but there's a pale light coming from somewhere. My clothes are dry. The space smells strongly of salt air and fish. I stand up, and as I walk through the thick layer of moist leaves, the sea odor grows stronger.

The tiny room is roundish and has no furniture except for a green orb of glass suspended shoulder-high in the air without any visible support. There's the faint sound of dripping water nearby. The light glances off the wall covering — my fingertips trace a fine network of gilded roots that snake over the rounded walls and ceiling. Just ahead is a black stone door, as glossy as a jewel, fixed in an ornate ring of silver. As I tiptoe toward it, the suspended glass orb over my shoulder moves with me, and I realize this is where the light's coming from.

Behind the black door's shiny surface, there are faint outlines of water flowers and twisted grasses. I step back and let out a little screech that echoes in the confined space when a large flat fish with spiky teeth swims through the shadowy glass and leers at me, then turns lazily and swims away.

Embedded in the outside of the glass, right at eye level, is a curious mass of dark silver that looks a bit like a two-headed sea horse. I touch it with my fingertip, and it splits in half and slides from view with a faint whoosh.

Light and deeply chilled air stream into the little room through the small opening, and with them comes two voices that I recognize immediately. I creep forward and peer through the opening. The room on the other side is dim, the vast floor as emerald and shiny as the tropical sea in my other dream. A huge fireplace made of the same black glass as the door stands against the wall to my left, and I'm sure I see movement behind its surface. In front of it, on a low couch, sits a small, slender woman, her silvery hair coiled so tightly and elaborately around her head it looks varnished. The loose flowing greenish garment she wears changes shade with every movement of her arm. She's embroidering on a piece of black fabric that glitters with silver fish and plants. Her right hand, which is holding the needle, is a bloodless gray, circled at the wrist with a jeweled bracelet, while the left, holding the fabric, looks normal. Flickers of shadow and delicate light undulate around the walls as if the whole room is under water.

A man stands near her. I suck in a sharp breath — *it's Huw*. The rings and jewels in his ears glint in the firelight. The left side of his face is still stained with the swirling blue tattoos, as are his bare wiry arms from fingertip to shoulder. His torso, long legs and feet are tightly covered in scaly green leather, and on his head is a wide sleek headpiece of feathers that seem to flow out behind him like the curious light that follows him everywhere.

I bite my bottom lip to keep from calling out to them — from demanding to know if they are real or a dream. Instead, I listen hard.

"Keir is demanding to come down," Huw says. "I've given him latifolia, felon and balm, but they've had no effect. He's out of control."

The woman looks up from her sewing. When she speaks, her strange synthesized voice echoes through the room. "I will *not* deal with his tantrums now. It's not my fault that he's been transformed for almost three moon crests. *You* have no power to change him back — nor do I. Only Mathus can do that. More important, tell me — this cave portal. Where does it go?"

"I still don't know, but I'm working diligently."

Rhona shakes her head. "Fergus may actually have us this time, Huw. By Ochain, I hope not!"

Huw says, "We'll beat him to the goal, my lady, once I pinpoint exactly where it is."

Rhona clenches the tapestry between her hands. "I *hate* Fergus for what he's done. He's got us chasing after some stupid child. Just to punish Keir because Keir was too impetuous with Fergus's silly little sister. It's ridiculous to begin a game where one hasn't even set a proper goal. It's like Fergus has gone mad, too!"

My stomach tightens. There's that word again. *Child.* What child?

Huw drops onto the couch beside her, shifting a pile of fine fabric and bowls full of silvery threads to one side.

"There's no doubt, my dear Queen Rhona," he says gently, "the game was set up in anger. And no doubt, Fergus has gone to where the child is stowed. Keir is at me all the time to solve the cave's cunning lock. My Readers are searching out this hot spot on their binnacles — to see where it leads. However, your brother wants to control the next move. He can't be allowed to. *I'll* solve the lock. *I'll* find Fergus — and through Fergus, the child, if it exists — and through *me*, you'll get control of Fergus's game."

She sighs. "Yes, of course you're right, Huw. But how *dare* Fergus promise the child's realm to Keir, then take it back. I'll see that Keir gets that island kingdom of Argadnel if it's the last thing I do. We'll beat them at the game. We'll get to the child first. I'm counting on you, my friend."

"Will you not consider sending Keir away for a while? For his own good."

She says plaintively, "I can't go against my own blood. Your tribe, the Blue Celtoi, clearly have no loyalties to kin. If you did, you would not be here with me, would you?"

Huw shakes his head sadly. "My people choose our loyalties on more important things than blood ties, my queen. Keir must be protected from his own recklessness. I don't trust any of your guards. I fear he'll talk one into releasing him. Then he'll try to break the cunning lock and, with his inexperience, may forge it shut instead."

"I trust my servants, Huw. And I won't imprison Keir far from me. Even so, I've warned him that he has used up my goodwill. He *listened*. Your job, as my Druvid, is to find Fergus, not to worry about my brother."

"Oh, I'll find him for you," Huw says fervently. "But I can't risk opening a portal as long as Keir could do damage. He could ruin any chance of —"

"My brother is a fool, but he doesn't deserve what they did to him ..." Rhona's voice lowers to a hiss. "If it takes a thousand years — I'll find Fergus. I'll make him pay. With the child's life — if it still lives. It wasn't *all* Keir's fault — Branwen played with his feelings. Fergus's sister has always been dangerously indulged. We have to find them. I will win this game!"

When she thrusts the needle through the fabric, she cries out, and a single drop of blood falls from her left hand into the center of a silver flower. "Look! An omen, Huw. Surely it's an omen. Blood will be spilt."

Huw opens his hand, and a lump of glass appears on his open palm, spins rapidly and turns into a strange fishlike creature, its long tail twisting in the air. In a high piping voice the little creature says, "On a crystal altar they'll lay him, with his spilt blood all around, and one will catch it in a palm, ere it reach the ground ..."

Rhona whispers, "*Him?* Keir ... Fergus?"

"A warrior will die ..." the voice proclaims, and the tiny creature vanishes.

I'm so caught up in the scene in front of me that I let out a squeak of alarm when a door on the wall behind Huw bangs open with a resounding crash, and a bizarre three-wheeled silver cart rumbles into the room. Two silver hounds lope alongside it, each wearing a collar studded with dark purple stones. The dogs from the cave. But it's the driver of the cart that makes my jaw drop. Its head, neck and upper shoulders are that of the sharp-toothed fish in the stone, sleek and glistening as if covered in oil, a long flapping tail hanging down its back. The fish head turns into the broad chest, arms and hands of a man, only to change into the twisted lower limbs of a goat, small hooves covered in boots of beaten silver. The creature is wrapped in a blue cloak decorated with silver shells. It's clear that he'd never be able to hold his weight up on his deformed legs.

The hounds ignore Rhona and Huw, and their slitted pale eyes fasten on my door. When they start to bray in unison, I'm certain they'll lunge at my hiding place, but the monster bellows at them, and they cower and slide around the cart on their bellies, whining loudly. Their large paws are webbed, with long thin nails, like platypus feet.

"What news, sister?" the creature booms in the deep choked-off voice that I recognize as Keir's.

My feet grow numb and a shiver like cold water ripples through me. I try desperately to concentrate on what's happening on the other side of the door, but a static crackle in the air distorts the sounds.

The creature's voice is loud, but broken, like a radio signal out of range. "… the right cave … Fergus's aura … *must* be the portal … demand it!" As I float past the opening, my breath light in my lungs, the last words I hear before I cut through the ceiling are, "… beat Fergus, Rhona … I will beat him!"

15

I'm relieved to find myself back in Albert's sitting room, the crystal held tightly in my hand. I have no burns on my fingers and I can't remember how I got back here, but I'm happy I didn't have to go through that scary green water again.

I shiver, thinking about the creature called Keir. Now I know why he was left behind in the first dream while the other two walked up to the cave where I was hiding. And why Rhona intends to make Fergus pay.

Did Fergus really turn him into that ugly man-fish because he went after his sister, Branwen? Is that what they meant by a cunning? Is real magic actually possible? Huw works for the queen as her — what had she called him — *Druvid?* Is a Druvid a magician? Will Queen Rhona really kill Fergus if she finds him? She says she'll kill the child, too. I wish I knew exactly who she was talking about. Maybe I could warn them. I hope, whoever they are, their hiding place is safe.

I shake my head. What difference does any of this make? It all comes from some twisted part of my brain. Yet it seems so real while it's happening. And even more curious is that the entire time I'm secretly watching and listening, I have this strange feeling of power over them, a power I might lose if I make contact with them.

I check my watch. Quarter to twelve. I feel a little shaky, but I'm really hungry. I finish the salad, but it isn't enough. When I wander into the kitchen, the door to the herbarium is open and there's a clinking sound coming from the room beside the greenhouse. I edge forward and take a peek. Janet is grinding something with a mortar and pestle. She reaches over and presses the button of a food processor, which whirs loudly. I back away. The last thing I want to do is talk to *her*.

The old man's tray is on the counter. I slide a piece of dark crusty bread out from under the plastic wrap and eat it quickly, then open the door to the stairs. I'm careful not to bang the walls this time, and when I get to the landing I use the edge of the tray to tap lightly on his bedroom door. No one answers. Maybe he's asleep. I put the tray down on a table in the hallway, turn the knob and peer in.

The bed is empty. The big sagging spot where the old man's enormous body usually lies is surrounded by a mess of books, papers and blankets. A pair of silk pajamas hangs over a chair beside the bed. I hope Albert doesn't expect me to help that gross old thing put them on. If he does, I'll leave and never come back.

The papers on the bed are heavy and cream-colored, covered in notes and mechanical drawings. In fact, upside down they look a lot like Dad's henge.

I put the tray down and am about to reach over to pick up one of the drawings when the corner of another sheet catches my eye. It looks like a pencil sketch of a small child — fine straight hair, part of an eyebrow and a rounded cheek. The tiny slice of face looks slightly familiar, but before I can slide the whole thing into view, a loud humming noise starts up behind a curtain on the far wall. Hair on end, I skitter across the room, down the stairs and straight into Janet.

She grabs my arm tightly. "What have you been up to?"

I twist out of her grip. "I was upstairs. Mr. Maxim isn't there. I came back down because I forgot his iced tea."

Janet's face looms closer, the heavy smell of cloves and damp soil engulfing me. For one startling moment, the yellow eyes change, the lids becoming saggy and inflamed, the irises a dull black; but when I step back, they're amber hard and narrow with suspicion. "Albert said you were to go up at precisely twelve o'clock, did he not?"

Standing this close, I have the feeling that she isn't solid — that if I push my hand against her, it will go right through. "I took Mr. Maxim his lunch a bit early, that's all," I say. "I thought he might like to play that board game afterward. I didn't do anything wrong. I'm in charge of looking after him. Not you."

She looks at me intently. "Still, rules are rules, are they not? In games as well as in life?" She laughs a deep throaty laugh.

I stalk past her to the kitchen, open the fridge and pour tea into a glass mug, then march back up the stairs.

"Twelve o'clock precisely," she growls after me.

"Twelve o'clock precisely," I mutter. Who does she think she is, complaining that I'm too *early* for work? Even so, I check my watch — when the big and little hands meet, I bang on the door.

"Come in," a familiar voice rasps.

The old man is in bed, dressed in the pajamas that were on the chair. "I see you've already been here," he says jovially, but there is something behind his eyes that isn't jovial at all. "I've got the afternoon all planned. First, lunch, and then let's see if you can beat my king, eh?" He points at the Fidchell board, rubs his hands together and chuckles deep in his throat. I don't like the sound of *that*.

16

We play Fidchell all afternoon. Every time I come close to getting a good lead on the king — all the while keeping my little band of players safe and herding them closer to the shore of the ocean — I'm convinced the pieces have moved without anyone touching them, and I have to figure out a new strategy. It's definitely more complicated than chess. A couple of times, I see alarm in the old man's eyes, so I know I'm better at the game than he expected — but at least he doesn't sweep the pieces off the board. He barely talks, grunting with pleasure when he slides into a secret cave or vanishes into a magic forest, pursing his lips and glowering whenever I skim past his army with my dwarf pieces in tow. Once, when his king is threatened, he actually growls.

The strangest part is how I feel playing the game — exhilarated, intense and definitely not myself. My heart beats faster, and my skin feels as if tiny electrical currents are rippling up and down it. It's like I'm actually running across the soft mossy floor of the forest dodging the bad guys, hiding my motley troop in a Dryad's hole, or suddenly flying above the king and his band of knights fighting their way out of a maze. I crouch in tree branches one minute, stalk the royal group the next or become a bush or a rock, and I can even make my small gang vanish for a few minutes at a time. It's hard but fun learning the magical powers I have when I'm the strange creature with the white hair and long pale hands and feet. And just like in my dream, I have that curious feeling of power over Poppy's pieces — power that I don't quite know what to do with. Not yet, anyway.

More than once, one of my hooded troop is captured and I have to go back and figure out how to rescue it.

Finally, late in the afternoon, my pulse goes straight up — I'm about to round up my whole team within half an inch of the shore. All I have to do is move them into a Leaphole and take them through a maze under the sea and we'll be safe. I've already outwitted the king's guards and locked them in secret dungeons. I move my pieces together onto the same space and, like magic, I figure out why they have such strange shapes. Their sharp angles and awkward contours slide together into a single piece — a tall cowled figure with such a beautiful face, it takes my breath away.

The old man's piggy eyes are furious, his cheeks an ugly red. His king is at least three moves behind us when I slide the cowled figure into the small hole that leads to the underwater maze. The old man stares at the board for a long time, then his face changes to a self-satisfied leer. From out of nowhere, one of his guards — who I'd earlier put in a small dungeon rather than killing him — escapes and moves diagonally across the board and cuts us off. This gives the king four free moves. He grabs the cowled figure from under the sea and the game is over.

The fat man's jowls have been shaking with anger, but his delight when I'm finally cut off by his guard is childish and loud. Although I'm angry at losing, his belly laugh infects me and we hoot like a couple of lunatics until my sides ache. Then we recap some of the other moves, which throws us into louder guffaws. I can't remember the last time I laughed like this.

"I'll get you next time," I warn, wiping my eyes.

He looks at me and grins gruesomely. "I doubt that, Sparrow. You surprised me once, but it won't happen again. I'm a practiced player but I under-estimated you. This was a fluke on your part."

I stop smiling. "I knew what I was doing."

"I don't think so. You should have killed that guard when you had him in your ken the first time. Too soft. That's what comes from not being trained early."

"What's that supposed to mean?"

"You've not been taught to be ruthless. Lost your nerve at the last minute. Real game players win at any cost."

"Who would want to be *ruthless?*" I huff. "Terrible people are ruthless. Isn't playing by the rules and having fun the most important thing?"

He shakes his head sorrowfully. "The whole point, my dear, is to *win*. Why play if you don't win? What else *is* there? And rules are only to protect the winner, not the loser. That's why we have so few of them. Without limits, one is all-powerful. And *that's* what makes playing the game so addictive ... so all-consuming."

"You make it sound like real life," I say. "Jeez, it's just a game."

His eyes flash. "But you see, my dear, the game is everything. *Everything*."

I try to get him to explain, but he smiles his Cheshire cat smile and closes his eyes. "I'm tired. It's almost six. Go home. But come back again. I enjoyed trouncing you and I'll enjoy doing it again."

"We'll see about that!" I snarl, but his loud snores drown me out.

I've been dismissed by the fat victorious king. I'm going to beat the socks off him next time.

17

I creep downstairs to avoid bumping into that horrible Janet person, but the silence on the main floor tells me I needn't have bothered. I pedal home on my rattling bike, my mind full of the strange events of the day. Two things are sure. One — I hate Janet. Something about her gives me the willies, even though she made my headache go away. And two — I love playing the game. I've never felt so ... alive before. It sure beats computer games. The old man was right about one thing — that game is addictive. I can hardly wait to get back to it. Thinking about the old man reminds me — where was he when I first entered his room? I wish I'd got a better look at the papers on his bed. Maybe tomorrow I'll ask him if I can see them.

I cruise up our driveway, park my bike against the barn and wander over to the house. The sky directly overhead is covered in enormous gray clouds edged with muddy yellow, while low-lying fierce black ones scud like miniature pirate ships along the horizon.

Dad and Mom are sitting at the kitchen table, a jug of cider between them. Every inch of table and countertop is covered in honey cakes shaped like overfed bees and old-fashioned rounded beehives. Summer is sitting on the window seat feeding pieces of a small cake to the cat. No sign of dinner for the humans, naturally, except for a few carrots on the chopping block.

Dad growls, "You didn't see Tom Krift on your way home, did you?"

Surprised, I shake my head. "No. Is something wrong?"

"I asked him to stay later this afternoon because I absolutely *had* to go into the city to get something. He refused, said he had to work for Albert Maxim from three to seven. When I got back half an hour ago the damn henge had been tampered with!"

"I've asked and asked, but they won't explain what *tampered with* means," Summer says sulkily. "They never listen."

"It means messed around with," I say.

"Oh."

"You think Tom did it?" I ask Dad.

"He worked hard earlier in the afternoon," Dad says vaguely. "I can't see him doing this if —"

"I told you not to let him hang around," I say.

Dad looks surprised. "Did you? Well, when I saw that Albert Maxim fellow in town a few days ago, he told me Tom was a good worker. Reliable. Strong."

I roll my eyes. "You can't trust him. I *told* you that."

"Lacey says he's really nice," chimes in Summer. "He lives near town."

I sneer. "*Nice?* You can't be serious."

Summer grins. "Maybe it's just you he isn't nice to! Maybe you've been bossing him around like you do us."

To divert her from any more silliness, I say to Dad, "What happened to your henge?"

He looks glassy-eyed. "I wonder if it could be my old nemesis, Jake Willfred. He was really upset when I got that national grant and he was passed over. Said he might drop by sometime and see what I was working on. I wouldn't be at all surprised if he —"

"Dad. What *actually* was done to your henge?"

"Or maybe I should have paid more attention to that note you found in the mailbox yesterday, Leto, and insisted that Tom stay at the site. That nonsense made me dismiss the whole thing as a hoax. This could be some crank from town."

"What's a hoax? What's a crank?" Summer asks, feeding the last bit of the bee's wing to the cat.

"What note?" I demand, knowing how hard it is to get my father to focus.

"What?" Dad looks confused. "Oh ... your mother found a note on a scrap of paper — warning me off my work on the henge. Said something about a child being the cause of everything."

"Are you *serious?*" I ask. "A child?"

Why is everyone talking about a child? Even in my dreams, Rhona and Huw talked about a child. But I can't tell my parents about the dream. It would sound crazy.

Mom gets up and starts peeling a carrot half-heartedly. "Some smart aleck put it in our mailbox. I told your dad to ignore it."

"What else did it say?" I try to sound matter-of-fact, but an alarm is going off inside me.

"That I had no right to build a circle henge," Dad says, "and if I continued the circle, the whole thing would be cursed."

I stare at them. "*Cursed?* No one says *cursed* anymore. And how can a pile of Plexiglas pieces in a cow pasture curse anything? It's got to be just kids fooling around." Am I trying to convince them ... or me? I'm sure this must be Tom's doing. But I have no proof. I need time to *think*.

"Doesn't cursed mean something bad?" Summer asks, and when no one answers, adds plaintively, "Doesn't anyone *ever* listen to me?"

"I'll tell you what's cursed, Summer," I say with a tight laugh. "Poor Grandpa MacFey's field. By that awful mess Dad's building on it. *That's* the only cursed thing around here."

If only that was true.

Mom is surprised. "Hey — I haven't heard you laugh in ages."

"Yeah ... well ... it's all so silly. Dad, you're getting paranoid again. Jake What's-his-name is probably in the middle of nowhere building a giant black fly he's going to call 'Oil Driller of the North' or something."

Dad thinks a moment, then says, "Listen, don't tell anyone else that idea. I like it. Your mom gave me the idea for my stone henge. Maybe I'll make your black fly next year."

I give up. "Mom, how did you know about Bruide Henge anyway?"

Mom blinks. "It came to me in a dream. Last winter sometime."

I lean forward. "A dream?"

She smiled. "I was walking in this strange foggy place and this ring of huge stones just kind of loomed up at me through the mist. I woke up immediately afterward — I was frightened and didn't know why. It wasn't until I was having my morning coffee that I remembered my dad once telling me about the village his people came from and this stone circle called Bruide Henge. He said something odd — about it being part of my future — whatever that meant." She smiles sadly. "I guess it must have gone deep into my psyche. Anyway, I told your dad about the old henge and he took it from there. Now I wish he hadn't. Maybe I should have talked him out of it."

"Why?"

She lifts one shoulder and looks at Dad. "I know the people around here. I should have realized it would cause a problem. They're very ... conservative, staid. They wouldn't want anyone making fun of their ancestors."

Dad sighs. "That's so silly. How can my henge be seen to be making fun of them, for Pete's sake? I'm honoring them, if you think about it."

I frown. "But ... how would the note writer even know that Dad's building a circle henge, anyway? It's not far enough along to look like much of anything."

"I didn't tell anyone," Summer says, as if she's been accused. "No one would understand what I was talking about. *I* don't even understand it. Besides, no one ever tells me a thing around here." She mutters that last bit to the cat, who lovingly licks crumbs off her hand.

Dad shrugs. "I might have mentioned it to a couple of people when I went into Bruide to buy a few things."

I flinch. "Dad ... you actually talked about the henge in town? They won't understand. They'll think you're ..."

"That I'm what? Crazy?"

"You said it, not me!"

"You still haven't told us what happened to the henge, Dennis," Mom says, giving me a warning look.

"The loose pieces were moved around topsy-turvy — two huge pieces of heavy Plexiglas. I have no idea how they did it. And there's —"

"But is anything actually damaged?" Mom insists.

"Just the panel I was working on, I think. And they filled in the part of my trench I haven't used yet. It doesn't make any sense. They don't appear to have touched the main structure — which is three-quarters done, Emma, and it definitely looks like *something*, thank you very much. It'll take me a few days to recut that piece, and I'll get Tom to dig out the section of trench. It'll slow me down, that's all. Maybe they think I'm planning on sacrificing someone on my circle's altar. They're so backward here, I wouldn't be surprised."

Mom says, "Hey, some of those backward people you're slandering had family that came over with my great-grandparents."

"Are you actually defending the townsfolk, Leto?" Dad asks in mock amazement. "You avoid going into town at all costs. You don't even like most of them. Take that Duncan MacIvor —"

"Dennis!" Mom warns, looking at Summer, who pipes up, "Lacey's dad? You don't like him, Mom? How come?"

"Of course I like him, honey," Mom says. "I knew him when I was a kid. I like his whole family and —"

Dad interrupts. "Well, whoever did it, it's still sabotage — *sabotage!* I can't keep guard twenty-four hours a day. I'll have to go into town and talk to a few parents, I guess."

"Dad, is building that thing worth all this hassle?" I plead. "Wouldn't it be better to paint pictures inside a studio or something? If it isn't the rain, it's dust and grit, and if it isn't dust and grit, it's getting people's backs up every time you start a new work. Look what's happened now. You've upset *someone* in Bruide!"

"Emma, you know I can't be shut in a studio doing stuff that's been done a million times before. I have to be —"

I'd heard it all before. "Yeah, I know … on the *cutting edge*. But, Dad, somebody's not happy. It could get worse. Why can't you stop for a while?"

He's not listening. He's loping out the door, his mind already in his cow field.

"Dinner will be in one hour," Mom calls out after him.

"I bet it was Lacey's brother and his friends *tampering* in Dad's field," Summer offers. "They got into trouble last Halloween *tampering*. Lacey said they put someone's old horse wagon on top of a barn roof, and no one could figure out how they did it."

Lacey's thirteen-year-old brother, Ryan, is one of the nicer kids around here. He doesn't tease me.

"I tutored Ryan in English before his finals," I say. "He wouldn't do something like that."

"Oh yeah?" she crows. "Well, him and some of his friends call you names behind your back."

"They do? What?" I ask, shocked.

"They call you a Pithwitchen. When I asked them what that was and if it was a bad name, Ryan kinda shrugged and said it was his parents who said you were a Pithwitchen. Mom? What's a Pithwitchen?"

Mom doesn't answer. She's a statue holding a carrot.

"Do you know what they mean, Mom?" I ask.

Now she's staring at the carrot as if she's never seen one before.

My stomach tightens. "Mom?"

She looks up but her eyes are focused on something inside her head. "Huh? Oh … Emma, I've got to go out for a few minutes … could you?" She holds up the carrot.

I take it from her, and she turns to Summer. "You're sure it was Duncan and Ina MacIvor who said these things?"

Summer nods. "Ryan said —"

"I'll be right back," Mom says, grabbing the truck keys from the hook and banging out through the screen door.

"What's wrong with her?" Summer asks. "Is she going to yell at Lacey's mom and dad for calling you names? I'm sorry I said anything. Are you mad?"

"Just shut up, Summer," I snap.

Above Summer's grumbling, I hear the truck start up. A few seconds later, it sweeps past the window, Mom hunched behind the wheel. Mom never drives to town. Is she really going to confront the MacIvors about what they called me? Why? I scrape unhappily at the carrot for a minute or so, then drop it on the table and head for the living-room bookshelves.

18

When Mom returns an hour later, she looks rattled and out of breath, as if she's been running instead of driving the truck.

"I made carrot soup for me. There's a salad — baked potatoes ready in the oven," I say. "You just have to fry the burgers. I want to talk about something."

Mom glances uneasily at Summer but she's sound asleep on the window seat.

"I looked up the word 'Pithwitchen' in the dictionary," I say quietly. "I couldn't find it. Then I looked at that funny old leather one of Grandpa MacFey's. I found it there. It means a kid with no parents. One who's secretly substituted for another child. Given to a childless couple. Also called a changeling. Comes from old legends, they say. The kids have tattoolike marks to distinguish them from real kids — marks in the shape of symbols — like suns and moons. These marked kids are given to the couple for a specific reason, but the reason is always secret. Why would Lacey's mom and dad call me a Pithwitchen, Mom?"

My mouth is dry, but I don't take my eyes off Mom's face. Her eyes are wide and unblinking. I hold my wrist in front of her face. "Look. Two crescent moons. Am I the child in that note you got? What did it say exactly?"

"Don't be absurd! What are you *talking* about, Emma?" She turns abruptly and slaps the burgers into the pan. "That is a *birthmark* on your arm. It *happens* to look like two moons. I should have had it removed when you were younger. I have no idea why anyone would say such a stupid and irresponsible thing. That note just said a child was the cause of *something*. But they didn't say what it was. Or who the child was. I don't even remember exactly what it said. It made no sense so we ignored it. So should you!"

"Where's the note?" I ask. "I want to take a look at it."

"I burned it."

"Why? If more vandalism happens, the police would want to see it."

Mom says in a flat tone, "I didn't think it meant *anything*. I still don't." She turns the burgers, but her movements are stiff and awkward.

"Where did you go in the truck?"

"Huh? Oh, I — uh — I just remembered I'd forgotten to pay for reserving my dad's old stall. They're very strict at the market."

"You didn't take your purse. How did you pay them?"

Mom stares at me. I think she's going to say something — admit something — but just then Dad storms in. "Can you believe it? One of my newly bonded Plexiglas stones has been wrecked. I didn't notice before. I have no idea *how* they did it. It would have taken brute force to do it."

"Then your henge is aptly named," Mom says.

He looks baffled for a second, then says, "Oh — right. Well, this piece is actually *twisted* out of shape. I'll have to make another one. It's *definitely* going to put me behind."

I watch Mom the whole time, waiting to see if she'll answer my last question, but she keeps talking to Dad in a loud, bright voice, telling him his bonding probably wasn't strong enough, and that's why the piece has fallen apart. Their mild arguing wakes Summer up, and the time for questions is over.

I can't eat my soup. Summer is pale and fidgety. Mom pushes her food around on her plate. Only Dad wolfs down everything in sight. I can feel Mom's eyes on me when I leave the house. I wait on the back stoop hoping she'll follow me out — explain where she really went, but when I look back through the screen, she once again starts talking animatedly to Dad.

The small black clouds have multiplied and taken over the sky. A heavy wind pushes against the willows, bending them to the ground. I walk through damp gusts that flutter my shirttails, past a row of beehives half hidden by long grass. A deep hum rises from the wooden boxes — a vibration I'm sure I can feel through the thin soles of my sandals. When I get up to my loft, I sit for a long time on my window seat watching the black clouds grow bigger and bigger.

Shaken by Mom's weird behavior and Dad's description of his twisted slab of Plexiglas, I grab my old journal and a pencil. Sometimes writing my thoughts down helps. I find a clean page and the first word I scribble is "child." Then I write "Pithwitchen" immediately below.

What did Lacey's parents mean when they called me a Pithwitchen? And what does my birthmark have to do with anything? I look at my wrist. The rounded sides of the crescent moons that face each other seem clearer than they've been before. The marks that were once dull pink have sharp bluish edges and seem slightly raised as if they've been freshly branded on my skin. Each little moon has a greenish cast. I run the tip of my finger over their soft, ridged surfaces, then write the word "moons." That makes me remember the two moons in the cave dream.

I randomly write "dreams," "Bruide Henge," "Plexiglas," "circle" ... and finally "Tom Krift," "Albert Maxim," "Poppy Maxim" and "Janet Krift." Then I draw a map showing Albert's field next to

Grandpa MacFey's cow field — marking where Dad's henge is located in the center. I plot out a couple of scenarios with Tom Krift acting as the villain, creeping up on my father's henge and "tampering" with it, while Albert is busy in another field. He could easily have done it.

I chew the end of my pencil. Under the drawing I write, "anonymous note." I can't believe that Ryan MacIvor's involved — Tom Krift is a much more likely suspect. After all, he's the one who hangs around Dad's henge, not Lacey's brother. It makes sense, but why would *anyone*, even Tom Krift, bother messing around with Dad's silly plastic henge? And how can a child be responsible for something? And *what* something?

I try not to let my mind veer too close to why Mom suddenly drove off like that. Something really serious happened in the kitchen, but I don't know *what*.

The wind outside moans loudly. Then without warning, the window above my bed crashes open and a stiff gust blows around the room like a mini-tornado, tearing at my hair and the pages of my journal. I leap to the window just as the owl flaps past, his heart-shaped ghostly face and pale eyes looking straight into mine. I wrench the window shut and push hard at the small bolt that holds it in place. At the same time, someone hammers on my door. I open it a crack.

"You okay, Emma?" Mom stands at the top of the stairs, her hair whirling around her head.

"I — I'm fine."

"Why don't you come to the house? Looks like a storm brewing."

"I'm okay, Mom. Really."

She looks worried. "You're sure?"

"I'm sure." I hesitate, then open the door wider. "Look, can we talk, Mom?"

"Can't now, sweetie, okay? Listen, if this gets worse I'm sending Dad up to fetch you," she warns, then runs down the stairs.

She makes it to the porch door just as a huge sheet of lightning splits over the prairie, showering it with light. More electricity flutters silently on the horizon. I shut the door and shatter into a million pieces when a deafening crack shakes the barn and something thunders onto the roof. Big white pellets of ice fly past, some bursting on the driveway, others jumping and banging into one another like bingo balls on the grass. The deafening roar goes on for ages, then drops down to a heavy rattle and finally into hushed silence.

"Emma?" Feet pound up the outside stairs.

Dad, holding a raincoat over his head, bursts in and gathers me up, and we crunch our way back to the house. Mom and Summer are waiting on the verandah.

"Wasn't that amazing?" Summer cries. She's curled up in a rattan chair with a knitted afghan tucked around her. Her eager face is as white as the crumpled balls of ice melting on the driveway.

"You okay?" I ask, a tiny catch in my throat.

"I had *another* fall-out right after you left."

I look at Mom accusingly. "That's two in two days."

"This time she fainted," Mom says, gently pushing Summer's hair off her forehead. "I'm taking her into town as soon as Doctor MacPherson returns from holiday. I won't go to his stand-in. He's useless."

"That Janet woman who works for Albert Maxim is supposed to be some kind of healer —" I say and instantly regret it "— but I don't think I'd trust her."

"Oh?" Mom asks. "What kind of healing does she do?"

"I don't know."

"Well, we'll see what Doc MacPherson has to say first, eh?" Mom replies in a low voice.

Seeing my sister's thin arms sticking out of the coverlet makes me sick with anxiety. I force myself to concentrate on what Dad is saying.

"... ten thousand golfers have all teed off at the same time." He's gazing through the screen. "Amazing."

"The quiet is almost creepy," Summer murmurs sleepily.

Dad nods. "It is. I thought it would rain after all that atmospheric fuss."

As we sit in a row, staring out through the screening, I hear something that makes me sit up. "Listen. Can you hear them?"

"Hear what?" Dad asks.

"The bees."

Mom looks at me warily.

"Look! It *is* the bees," Summer cries, pointing.

A small black cloud of them hovers over the hives closest to the barn. Then it separates, rises and joins again in a single vibrating mass.

"My god," Mom says, pressing against the screen. "Something's happened."

"What?" Summer asks. "Have their homes been wrecked with the hail?"

Dad squints. "The hives look intact. What do you mean, Leto?"

"My father always said that when the bees swarm in the evening, especially after a storm, there's trouble brewing."

"What kind of trouble?" I ask.

Mom's eyes are intent on the cloud of insects. "I don't remember. He was always going on about omens and signs, but I wasn't all that interested. It was only when I was older that I —" She chews her bottom lip and looks anxiously out the screen.

"Are they dangerous?" I ask. "Because, if not, I'd like to go back to the barn."

"Wait," Mom says. "I'll be right back."

We watch her walk toward the swarm of bees. Standing a short distance away, she speaks to them in a low, almost crooning voice. Above her, the clouds have reshaped into heavy soot-dusted beasts that randomly growl. The humming of the swarm drones ominously but Mom keeps talking. When a cold wind sifts through the screen, like magic, the swarm shrinks and vanishes.

Mom runs back to the house.

"What did you do?" we all ask at once.

"I did what my dad used to do when the bees acted up. I talked to them. And it worked!"

"Wow!" Summer breathes. "It was like magic, Mom."

Mom looks flushed and very pleased with herself. "It felt a bit like magic, too, honey. Now, let's take you inside the house. It's getting cold."

"I only hope this hail hasn't damaged my crystal," Dad says. "I stupidly left it over at the henge. Oh well, I don't imagine any pranksters will be messing around tonight, right?"

"I'll make a run for the barn," I say. "Got to get up early for work."

"I'd rather you stayed in the house tonight," Mom says, frowning. "I don't like this wind — it feels wrong. There's a lot of electromagnetism in the air."

"She'll be fine." Dad lifts Summer in his arms.

"But, Dennis, I can feel the dynatrons —" Mom almost never worries about me. Now she's practically wringing her hands because I'm going to cross the yard.

I push open the screen door and call out, "I'll be fine. I'll see you tomorrow."

I run past the now silent beehives, up the barn stairs and into my room, where I drop onto the window seat and stare miserably into the dusk for a long time. Everything seems out of whack. Nothing feels right. A large moth flutters against the window, its tattered wings tapping the glass. The poor thing must have got injured in the hail storm. I begin to worry about the owl. Did it make it to safety before the hail hit? I crawl through the flap door and peer into the shadows. When my eyes adjust to them, I can make out the owl's pale silhouette resting on a broken board jutting out from the old hayloft. Before I can slide onto the beam, the owl shakes itself, stretches its wings and flies slowly away from its perch. As it drifts down to the barn floor, the night air shimmers and slides around it — like a skip-stone breaking the surface of still water. Its wings swirl and flutter, then suddenly everything grows hazy, as if the darkness in the barn has moved behind my eyes. When it clears again, the bird is gone and a man stands on the concrete floor below.

I know instantly who it is. And this time he isn't going to get away.

19

I dash down the stairs, run to the front of the barn and get there just as Tom Krift, dressed in jeans and a T-shirt, comes out the side door.

"What are you doing here?" I shout.

"Oh — hi," he answers casually, but I know I've startled him.

"If you don't tell me exactly what you were doing in my barn, I'm going straight to my father and he'll call the RCMP. Did you hurt my barn owl? Where is he?"

"Of course I didn't hurt him. I was bird-watching. I didn't realize you were in the barn or I wouldn't have gone in."

"I don't believe you."

"Look, you have a barn owl. I'm interested in owls. It flew out of the barn just a second ago. I bet you don't even know that the barn owl is endangered. All because you people insist on poisoning mice. The owls eat dead mice and they die."

"What do you mean, *you people?* I don't use poison. Neither does my family. I like owls. I particularly like *my* barn owl."

He grins. "He's quite a bird, isn't —?"

"Never mind that! What are you up to? Were you here during the hailstorm?"

"Yeah. Some show, huh? Hey, did you know you've also got a burrowing owl nesting in that small wood across the road? They're endangered, too. Your father gripes constantly about groundhog holes. If he decides they're a problem in the field where he's working and puts down poison, that'll put an end to that little owl, as well."

I push my head forward, hands on my hips. "My dad wouldn't do that and you know it! I saw you running across my yard last night, you know. This is *not* about owls!"

"Come and see, if you want," he says, waving a hand toward Grandpa MacFey's wood. "I can show you the burrowing owl right now."

"Owls schmowls!" I snarl. "I bet that was you who messed around in my father's field, wasn't it? Why did you ruin his Plexiglas stone?"

Tom narrows his eyes and wraps his thick arms across his chest. "So, someone messed with the henge circle after I left, eh?"

"Yes. You!"

He shrugs. "Could be anyone. Everyone knows what your crazy father's building. What's he trying to do? Call up the ancient spirits. Hey, maybe he called up that hailstorm." He laughs harshly. Before I can answer, he adds, "If you don't want to check out the owl, I'll get a move on."

"You don't know anything about my father! Or me!" I shout at his retreating back. "And stay away from my barn! And my house! And my family!"

He strides across the road and plunges into the wood.

A new wind suddenly pushes me forward. Without another thought, I run after him.

20

I stop in the middle of the road and stare at Grandpa MacFey's wood. The stiff breeze is cold on my bare arms. A low ceiling of clouds races past overhead. Now and again, the pale eye of the moon blinks out, its light bouncing off the fluttering willow leaves.

I slide forward, making sure the gate doesn't creak as I drag it open and step into the wood. Just ahead of me, a twig cracks like a pistol shot. I quickly start toward the sound, all of my senses charged. At the same time, there's a flicker of something, a memory — of hidden places, of hideaways deep inside shadowy caverns. I'm not sure what it is — a smell, a sound, a darting movement, but I suddenly stop dead in front of a small sapling with a curiously twisted trunk. I don't remember this tree — or the two paths, one along either side of it.

Something is wrong … out of synch … as if everything in the wood has stopped to take a breath. The pressure swells in the air. My skin expands and my nostrils seem to open deep into my throat, taking in the rich fruitiness of moist earth, the dense acid of crushed leaves underfoot and another smell I can't identify but that makes the hair on my arms prickle.

I walk softly down the left-hand path. Surely it leads to Dad's field. But the dim shape of the twisted little tree suddenly pops up in front of me, the same two paths on either side. Have I walked in a circle? Gritting my teeth, I plunge down the right-hand path. The moon melts along it, leading the way, but a few minutes later I'm once again standing in front of the twisted tree. I turn around. I'll go back to the farm the way I came. I follow the moonlit path searching for familiar markers, but I can't see any. Nothing is familiar. Nothing. My pulse clicks higher. I walk and walk — and once more I land in front of the twisted tree.

Stay in control. It's dark and you're confused, an inner voice warns me. *If worse comes to worst, you can wait until morning and then find your way out. Just keep calm.*

"I swear, if I see you one more time," I snarl at the little tree, "I'll come back tomorrow and hack you down." I plunge along the left path again, only to land at the tree once more.

It's as if the wood has turned into a maze, just like on the Fidchell board, and all paths lead back to this tree.

I take a deep shuddering breath, close my eyes and listen to the silence. I'll pretend that I'm the pale little creature I played in the Fidchell game. It can't be any harder to get out of here than it was to find my way through a complicated maze on the board. Slowly the clicks and creaks and rustlings of the forest return. I close my eyes and imagine the layout of the little wood. I trace the way to Dad's field in my head. I open my eyes. I'll ignore the two paths. I walk up to the little tree and slide around it. Suddenly the old familiar path appears on the other side. It's then that I feel as if I'm being watched ... as if each step I take, someone takes a step with me. The hairs on the back of my neck prickle. I look over my shoulder now and again, but see nothing.

A few minutes later, the familiar opening appears through an arch of trees — I've reached Dad's field! In the moonlight, his circle shimmers — organically shaped hollow blocks of opaque Plexiglas, etched here and there with Celtic symbols, wooden beams stretched between them. Wow, he's right — it's actually becoming a henge.

Still with the uneasy feeling of being spied on, I start across the field but quickly dodge behind a tree. Two men are standing near the henge. Neither is wearing a white T-shirt. Who are they? Something moves in the corner of my eye — a small woman walks toward the two men from the direction of the river, her long dark hair shining like polished mahogany in the silvery light. She's wearing an ankle-length dress of russet brown that flutters like autumn leaves with every step.

I watch her shimmer across the field to the men. Then with tightly held breath, I run over an open patch of field to a clump of burnished bushes. Crouched behind them, I can see the two men better. They're both dressed in dark clothes, one tall and broad with a bald head, the other short and stocky, a wild mop of dark hair floating around his head.

"Well, Mathus. What news? Will it work?" the woman calls out in a deep lilting voice.

"We just got here ourselves, Branwen," the bald man says. "Tamhas was to be watching the site."

"Did you call him away to do another of the thousand errands you've given him, Fergus?" she asks.

The shorter man growls, "If you've only come to goad me, Branwen, you can go away!"

She laughs. "Tamhas *should* be here with you, Mathus. I don't trust my dear brother as he's not as experienced as you two are in these things, even if he *is* responsible for this whole fiasco. Has Tamhas repaired it? Is that what caused the storm? Perhaps it's been breached. Are *they* here as well? If we could blunder through, why not them?"

"As always, too many uninformed silly questions, sister dear," the one she called Fergus calls out. "We may have blundered through, but as I've told you a dozen times, Mathus has successfully blocked both sides until we can prepare it properly."

The bald man, Mathus, says, "The storm was probably just an accidental aside. There's too much energy. We have to set up a suppressant. Tamhas will do that."

"Can one block anything from Huw once he's determined to find a way through, Mathus?" she asks him. "And *will* it work for us? Will we be able to go home again?"

Mathus answers, "We're having difficulties but it'll work. I'll see to that! This Sweeney has constructed a monstrous elaborate gate like the Old Ones made. As even you can tell, its energy is out of whack."

I sit back on my heels, stunned. Fergus? Mathus? Branwen? Aren't those the names from my dreams? And who is this Tamhas? Am I sound asleep now — perched high above the barn floor? Was even the hailstorm a dream?

The smaller man, Fergus, speaks in a brisk, firm tone. "We can't wait much longer or the child will die. And there's the Watcher — it could take it and disappear."

Branwen sounds petulant, but echoes my thoughts, "Why won't you tell me *who* this child really is? As for the Watcher, surely it's not capable of *feelings*. Bargain with it. Why is this *child* so important? Why can't you tell me? After all, brother, I *am* a member of your team."

The *watcher?* I glance over my shoulder. Is that who was following me?

Fergus snaps back at Branwen, "You're not a member of anything. You tagged along — and you'll know what I decide to tell you."

"But when?" she cries. "I'm so *bored*. I want the game to either get going or just *end* so I can go home!"

Fergus holds up one hand. "Whist!"

My heart stops when a sudden gust of cold wind flattens the willow bush where I'm hiding. But they aren't looking at me. They're staring at something in the middle of Dad's henge, something that fills the circle with an unearthly luminous light. In the opening between the frosted Plexiglas stones, Dad's amethyst is hovering in the air as if held up by an invisible string.

"That fool Sweeney has put a channeler on the site!" Mathus shouts. "That could forge the portal shut. Where the devil is Tamhas? He should have seen it!"

Branwen cries, "It's turning red!"

Fergus charges toward the henge. "It could be Huw! Breaking the cunning lock!"

Mathus calls out, "Don't touch it! Sire!"

Branwen runs after the two men, but before they can reach the center of the circle, Tom Krift appears from the bushes to my right, races toward the crimson glow, plucks the crystal out of the air and holds it like a football under one arm. I smell something horrible as he dashes past me aiming for the river. I run after him.

"Look. It's the girl!" someone shouts.

Tom is face down in the shallow river, the stink of burned flesh rising from the foaming water. I reach out to help him, but someone pulls me back.

"Let go!" I shout, kicking out. "Tom's hurt!"

"Ow! I can't hold her!" the woman cries.

I shove her off me and reach for Tom's shoulder, but stronger hands lift me away.

"Tom!" I call, straining my neck to see him.

"Enough!" Fergus strides toward me. He's in smooth brown leather, like a biker, tooled all over with a greenish swirling pattern. Around his neck is a thick gold band open at the front where a pair of wolf heads wrought in dull gold glare at each other. His hair is loose and wild, his features flat and hard. A deep scar slithers down his right cheek like a snake. But it's his eyes that unnerve me — jet black with no whites showing.

"Let her go, Mathus," he commands.

"Who — who —" is all I can manage, because as soon as Mathus loosens his grip, I take off.

I fly past Dad's tent, past the henge, the earth tipping and shuddering in front of me. I focus hard on the fence as it draws near. In slow motion I reach out for the fence rail, but instead of grabbing hold of the weathered wood, my fingers wrap around a handful of cloth, my knuckles pressed against the hardness of muscle.

"No —" I gasp.

"It's okay, Emma."

Tom slowly eases my hand away from his T-shirt. I stare at his rough face in wonder. Behind him, water glints in the moonlight. I've run full circle and ended up back at the river.

"Are you okay?" he asks.

I lift both his arms, search his hands for burns, then touch his shirt and feel the healthy warmth of his body through the dry cloth.

"But — but you were hurt," I say.

He lowers his face to mine. "Really? Did that upset you?"

"I — I saw some people. They were — you were … I thought you were dead."

He looks puzzled. "Well, I must have nine lives then — like a cat. I saw you moving like a stiff-legged ghost around the field. Then you started to run. I barely caught up. You were sleepwalking, I think."

I blink at him. "Sleepwalking?"

He grins. "More like sleep *running*."

My head buzzes. Have I been asleep this whole time? Is he telling me the truth? I didn't actually see those people? But I *know* I did. Yet I *couldn't* have. Tom was seriously hurt. Now he's standing right in front of me, as sturdy as ever.

"I — I've got to get home," I mutter, not knowing what else to say.

"I'll walk you."

I shrug. Suddenly I'm so exhausted I can hardly speak.

We start up the slope from the river. As we pass by the henge, someone moves through the smaller trees at the edge of the forest, someone who flutters like moonstruck autumn leaves.

I point, my hand shaking. "See? She's there."

Tom squints around. "I don't see anyone."

The figure slides in and out of the trees. "There. See? Over there ... the woman. Branwen!" I lunge forward, but he grabs my arm in a firm grip.

"No one is there, Emma."

I turn and trudge toward the fence. He doesn't believe me. Why should he? I'm tired, so tired. When I reach the fence, I can barely crawl over it.

"Are you going to help Albert at the market on the weekend?" he asks.

It takes me a minute to remember who Albert is, my brain is so muddled. "No, I have to help my mom."

"You'll be careful, okay?"

I straddle the top of the fence railing and stare at him. "What's that supposed to mean?"

He hesitates, looks over his shoulder, as if trying to locate something, then says, "I think you should know ..." He stops.

"Know what?" I'm not tired anymore. I leap down on the other side of the fence and stare at him over the railing.

"You aren't who you think you are," he says.

"What's that supposed to mean!"

He hops over the fence. "I'm sticking my neck out here, and I don't even know why. So quiet down."

I whisper fiercely. "*Tell me.*"

"You watch your family all the time, don't you? To make sure they're safe. Right? That's your job — that's how you see it, right?"

"I suppose … well, yes. So?"

"How many kids lie awake keeping watch over their families like you do?"

"I don't know. I've always had trouble sleeping."

Tom holds up his hands as if pushing himself away from me. "I can't say anything more except … keep *watching*. If you see anything that doesn't seem right … if you think you or your family is in any trouble, think of me — I mean really *think* about me and — well, that's all." He runs his hand through his hair and moans, "I don't have any idea why I'm doing this!"

My scalp tightens. "You're just trying to scare me. What kind of trouble?"

"You'll know. You're a Watcher. Like me. That's our *purpose*."

Why is he calling me that? "What do you mean … a *watcher?*"

"Maybe you should talk to your parents. About the Keeper — your grand-da."

"My what?"

"Your grandfather. He chose you, after all."

I grab his arm. "Chose me? What do you *mean*."

He gently releases my hand. "I can't tell you. Perhaps your mother will know — but she didn't stay with your grand-da as she should have, so perhaps she doesn't know after all."

"Why should she have stayed?" I ask. "What do you know about my grandfather? Why do you call him the Keeper?"

His face closes down and he starts to walk away, then stops and says, "Just be careful. Go home."

"Careful of what?"

"Be alert, Emma," he says, then on a breath of air I think I hear something that sounds like "little Creirwy." Whatever that means.

When I reach the mouth of the farm's driveway, I look back. He's standing on the same spot, shuddering in the moonlight like a road mirage on a hot day, as if he's no longer solid.

I trudge down the gravel road to the farm. The lights in the house are out. It doesn't matter. I'll wake them up if I have to. I need answers. *Now.* Overhead, I hear the soft whoosh of wings. The owl is returning to the barn.

21

Mom's alone on the verandah, sitting close to the screen.

"I thought you'd be in bed," I say.

Her voice is low, uneasy. "I've been waiting for you. You shouldn't go out alone into the wood at night. I saw you with someone. Who was it?" Her eyes glint in the darkness.

"Tom Krift. He knows about an owl in the wood. We went looking for it."

"Did you see it?"

I shake my head, open the screen door and walk into the verandah.

Mom doesn't look at me, but past me out into the darkness. "About today … earlier, I mean. There are some things that I — I'm not sure about, but … after Summer went to bed, I spoke with your dad — he wanted both of us to talk to you together."

Dad bumps through the door carrying a tray with three glasses of lemonade. I put mine on the windowsill. I can't swallow anything.

"You want a light on?" Dad asks.

"No."

Mom leans forward and takes my hand. "About what Summer said earlier tonight."

I slide my fingers away and in a dead voice say what I already know to be true. "Tom Krift said Grandpa MacFey chose me. I was adopted, right? Everyone knows but me ... that I'm this Pithwitchen ... this *changeling*. Are either of you my parents?"

Dad lets out a low groan, pulls me close and hugs me hard. "Oh, Emma, we've had you since the day you were born. You're our daughter. I'm sorry we didn't tell you before this."

I step out of his arms. "The point is, you're not *really* my parents, right?"

My chest hurts from holding all this anger and fear inside.

He takes a deep breath. "Your mom had a hard time getting pregnant. We'd given up hope. Then finally, to our delight, she was able to conceive. She felt she *had* to come home in her ninth month, so she could be near her dad. He'd asked especially, and Leto couldn't say no —"

Mom interrupts. "It was more than that. It was ... I don't know ... a kind of incomprehensible spiritual *need* to come back."

Trust her to lapse into mumbo jumbo when she's trying to talk about feelings. I guess my face shows her what I'm thinking because she adds, "I must have known you were waiting for me here."

"Things don't happen like that," I say.

Dad clears his throat. "In any case, I agreed to bring Leto to the farm as long as she promised to have the baby in a hospital in Winnipeg. We drove for days. Maybe the drive was too … grueling … well … she lost the baby as soon as she got here. I blamed the old man. He blamed me. It was pretty tense."

Mom lets out a small sob. "My father tried to make it better. He *did*. We'd had our differences — he'd tried to force me to remain here, but I'd made my own choices. This time he didn't actually *force* me to come … I felt I could — *should* — come … Then it all went wrong!"

I stand separate, my back pressed against one of the porch posts. Fireflies blink on and off in the grass beside the verandah. Exhaustion sweeps over me again, making me breathless. I'm so tired.

Dad continues in a shaky voice, "Your grandfather was as upset as we were. That night he came home and said a young girl staying in Bruide had just given birth to a baby. The local midwife attended that delivery, too. The mother was very young and was going to give up her child for adoption. When she heard — from the midwife — what had happened to us, she offered us her baby."

My throat is as tight as a clenched fist, but I manage to say, "Who was the mother?"

"We never found out. Your grandfather brought you home within hours of Leto losing our baby. I was against it — I argued, but he brought you anyway.

And, oh Emma, as soon as I saw you, I knew you were ours. Your mom and I both did."

"But I'm *not* really, am I?" I say. "I've always known I was different — apart. The watcher."

The word echoes through my head again and again. *Watcher, Watcher, Watcher.* Tom Krift called me a watcher. And the people in the field used the word, too. I try to remember what they all said about watchers, but my head is a muddled mess.

"Watcher?" Mom asks. "That's what my dad called you when —" Her eyes widen, only the whites visible in the shadowy light. She stumbles to her feet and hugs me, and when I don't respond, she tightens her hold, her body trembling. I should comfort her — tell her it's okay, but I can't.

"Were you ever going to tell me I wasn't yours?"

In a voice thick with tears, Mom whispers, "I felt we didn't have to. You *were* my baby. You *are* my daughter."

I shake my head and say sadly, "No, Mom. *Summer* is your daughter. I'm not even legally yours, am I? I mean, it doesn't sound like there were lawyers or papers, right?"

When neither answer, I say, "So I'm nobody's daughter." I walk out into the cool night. Mom is crying and calling my name, but I hear Dad say, "Give her some space, Leto. It's a lot to take in."

I make it to my little room above the barn. I know how upset they are, but I can't do anything to make it better. I can't even help myself. Nothing feels real. Nothing can ever be the same again. I undress like a robot and crawl under my duvet. It's harsh and cold against my skin. I lie in the dark staring at the smoke-colored beams. All around me is a dark thrumming loneliness and a sadness so deep it melts my bones. My skin feels as thin and fragile as a tattered moth's wing. A touch will shatter me into nothingness. If only I could vanish. No more pain. No more sadness, just … nothing.

Someone knocks softly on my door and it creaks open before I can tell them to go away.

"Emma? You awake?"

Summer stands on the threshold in her pajamas, her bare feet blue with cold.

"What are you doing here?" I snarl, anger that surprises me pushing up past the numbness.

"I had to see you."

"Go to bed. You'll catch pneumonia standing there."

Summer says, "I heard."

"Heard what?"

"Everything. I listened to Mom and Dad talking about what to say to you. Then I heard them tell you."

"It doesn't matter, Summer," I say, my voice dull with pain.

She opens her mouth as if to say something, but bursts into tears.

"Summer, just go back to bed, okay?"

"B-but don't you see — it's all my fault. I don't deserve to ... to *liiive!*"

"You're freezing. Come and warm your feet up, then go!"

She remains by the door, wailing. "I — I deserve to be cold! I deserve to freeze into a big lump of ... of ice with frozen lungs and a frozen brain and a frozen great big mouth! If it wasn't for me, you wouldn't know ... about *you know!*"

Sobbing loudly, she throws herself at me. I smile. I can't help it. Somehow, in all the drama, things seem more normal. Not a lot. Just a bit.

"They love you so much," she says, her voice muffled in the comforter. She presses her hot face to mine. "And I love you a whole lot even though we fight sometimes. You — you won't go away will you? You'll stay with me? You — you *have* to!"

"I wouldn't leave you," I say. And it's true. I can never leave her, leave them. I have to watch over my family. Tom was right — that's my *purpose*.

22

After I take Summer back to the house, I sit on the window seat until the sky turns pale yellow. Everything that's happened in the last two days goes through my head. I know dreams can't be real. But Tom Krift seems to think my family is threatened in some way. My fears aren't unfounded. But how? Why?

I take the crystal out of my pocket. If I go back to Queen Rhona's world, will I hear more about the child ... me? Whether or not it's a fantasy doesn't matter anymore. What does *anything* matter anymore? I look at my birthmark. The blue edges are wider now, covering nearly all of the crescent moons, the tiny centers a dull green. It's as if they are being slowly injected with colored dye. With a recklessness that both frightens and excites me, I press the crystal against my wrist, praying I won't end up in that sea again, but in the small room beside Rhona's.

It happens exactly as I hoped — I wake up in the damp little room with the seaweed floor. I scramble to my feet and touch the silver sea-horse creatures on the door and peer through the opening into the cold dim space beyond. Queen Rhona is pacing the shiny floor with a stiff-legged gait, dressed in a flowing cloaklike dress of deepest blue, a high flame-colored collar around her neck, her hair held by an elaborate, twisted-silver headpiece that fits over the entire back of her head and sweeps past her face into winglike shapes that glitter with purple stones. Huw stands beside the huge fireplace, tossing chunks of what looks like black ice onto a crackling fire and rubbing his hands together. Each movement is echoed by the eerie light that follows him. He seems breathless, as if he's just arrived. He's dressed in a long coat made of small pieces of silver encrusted with gold shells — a round billowing hood covered with short red spines covers his head and shoulders. He pushes it away.

"They've gone to Eorthe."

"Eorthe?" Queen Rhona cries in her strange robotic voice. "Huw — are you sure?"

"I have been to the Readers. I used all of my powers. That's what I saw. Madam, we have to keep this to ourselves. I have grave concerns about Keir. I've heard disturbing things."

"Mere rumors," she snarls.

"My spies tell me he is trying to gather a team — to become rogue players in Fergus's game. If Keir gets wind of what we know —"

"Keir is loyal to me."

"He is dangerous, my queen."

"Be careful what you say about my own blood, Druvid," she snaps.

"Madam, with all respect, Keir is the cause of this conflict between you and Fergus. If you are to win Fergus's game, your brother must *not* disobey his queen."

As Rhona paces back and forth with her halting, almost mechanical gait, the high collar suddenly twists around her head like a bright flame — yellow and orange and magenta with streaks of blue that flash and sputter like sparklers.

"He will *not* try to usurp my position in the game! I won't listen to any more idle gossip!"

Huw bows, but the look he gives her is one of pity.

"Trust Fergus to choose a place where no one has been for eons," she snarls. "He's a clever player, but he must have known we'd find out."

Huw sighs. "You're both powerful rulers, madam. Together you would have commanded a huge kingdom that would have made the game even more exciting — you could have expanded it into uncharted realms. You could have power over the seas, Fergus command over the forests. Madam, think what you could still do together if you will only mend this rift. The possibilities are endless. Why fight over a little kingdom like Argadnel when there are massive kingdoms with huge bounties to conquer? It's not too late."

"Never!" The colors flare behind her head like a silk fan.

"Don't forget, madam. Fergus is a strong adversary. He has many players. Shrewd, artful, slippery and wild. And all are fiercely loyal. You don't have to go up against them. Fergus would forgive you — if not your brother."

The silver shells on her sleeves tinkle merrily, belying the fury in her voice. "And *you* must understand, Huw. I don't need to be forgiven. Nor does Keir. One of Fergus's pledges on our betrothal was to give Argadnel to Keir. That would have allowed Keir the freedom and power he craves. He could have slowly wooed other small kingdoms to play against him — and left Fergus and me to make challenges worthy of our new magnitude."

"Keir never plays by the rules. He —" Huw begins.

"No! It was Fergus who broke his promise to Keir and set this game into play! I will win Argadnel for my brother. It's his *right*."

Huw's lip curls. "And you really think that little kingdom will satisfy Keir, madam? He *deliberately* set out to end this great alliance between you and Fergus. He tried to kill Branwen when she spurned him. He plotted to turn Fergus's warriors against him. He wants both your kingdoms — yours *and* Fergus's. His bloated ego blinds him to the fierce loyalty of Fergus's people, but he is building up a strong base in Fomorii — with your own people. Don't blind yourself to this, I beg you."

Rhona halts directly in front of him and hisses, "He knows his place. I have his word on it. But what I do wonder about is your loyalty, Huw, when you slander my own blood."

Huw bows deeply in a sweeping glow of light. "Forgive me, madam. My only concern is for my queen."

She turns her back to him and says, "And your queen is so filled with hate and revenge that it fairly chokes her."

"It's still not too late —"

She holds up her hand. "Enough! Wasn't it *I* who swallowed my pride and begged Fergus to give Keir the island kingdom of Argadnel? And wasn't it Fergus who betrayed *me?* Now he's going to get this stupid orphan child and put *it* on the throne? Not while I still draw breath!"

Huw speaks slowly and evenly. "The death of the false king of Argadnel, the child's uncle, has come as it was foretold. The people of Argadnel want the rightful king's child to lead them. Fergus has kept this child hidden — and would have continued to do so, if only Keir had conducted himself as a true Knight of the Fomor. Had he done so, Fergus would have convinced the people of Argadnel to accept Keir. But instead —"

"No more!" she cries. "I know what Keir did. It's strategy we need, not reprisals. We know the portal

Fergus used. You'll soon open it …" She looks at Huw with a sneer. "… unless you think Mathus's cunning lock is beyond your skills."

Huw's brows gather into a thick line. "I *will* decipher his code, madam, and I'll bring the child to you. They won't even know it's gone."

"And I'll go with you."

"That's impossible."

"I'm the queen of Fomorii!"

"Madam, we could become stranded in Eorthe for some time if the return portal has been dismantled. Who knows what Keir could get up to here with you gone?"

She looks ready to argue, but then nods. "Yes. I'll wait here for a while then, but not long. Break the code and I will reward you well."

"My only reward will be your favor, madam," Huw replies, his black eyes glinting in the firelight, but when she turns away, his expression changes to amused disdain.

I want to hear more, but their voices fade. The small window in the door blurs. With a breath-sucking lurch, my feet leave the ground and like a spearhead I cut right through the ceiling of the little room into a space luminous with light the color of bay leaves. The pressure in my ears is like I'm swimming deep under water. When the green changes to the palest of lime, then to cold clear crystal, I surge to the surface with a blissful gasp.

23

I open my eyes and stare wildly around. I try to sit up, but which way is up? I'm sure I'm in my room, but the windows are in the wrong place. I blink hard, the room rights itself and I flop onto my bed. My pajamas are damp — more like I've been sweating than fighting my way through a pale green sea.

The morning sun has crept over my windowsill. Where *is* this place I go that is half dream, half real? Why was I able to go straight there this time, but still had to fight my way up through all that water to get back? Where is the place called Eorthe that Rhona and Huw talk about? Eorthe? I say it out loud. "Eorthe" sounds … are they saying *Earth?* I sit up again, alert and tingly. Rhona called herself the Queen of Fomorii. A place beside a huge green ocean with purple sand? I've never been great in geography, but even I know there's no such place on Earth. Besides, didn't she talk about dozens of other worlds that Fergus may have traveled to? Where are these worlds? And what is the game they keep talking about?

It's just another stupid dream, I remind myself. These bizarre people aren't from anywhere except my own out-of-control imagination. Something else begins to niggle its way into my overheated brain. I veer away from it, but it squeezes in like sticky honey through a crack and I remember what I want to forget.

Mom and Dad. And Summer. My family that isn't my family.

A dull ache grips my chest. Why can't the conversation with Mom and Dad turn out to be a dream — a nighttime fantasy I can wake up from?

But it's only too real.

My fingers fumble with the buttons of my shirt. I don't want to go to Albert Maxim's, but I can't stay home — I can't face Mom or Dad. I finish dressing, shove an old baseball cap into my pocket and run down to get my bike. Just as I wheel it around the corner of the barn, Mom comes out of the house.

"You didn't come in for breakfast, so I figured you'd slept in." She hands me a bag. "I made some scones." Her voice is bright but her eyes are swollen.

"That's why the bag's so heavy," I say automatically. Mom's rock-hard biscuits are a family joke.

Her smile is uncertain, and when I don't respond, it slides off her face. "We've — uh — we've made quite a mess of this haven't we — your dad and I?"

I shrug. "I gotta go to work."

"Emma, love, I know we should have told you ... but you are so much a part of us — that first moment we held you — it was as if ..."

"As if you were holding your *real* baby," I say. "The one that died."

"The second you were put in my arms, you were *my* child." Her words hang between us like tattered bits of cloth.

"You should have told me, Mom."

"I don't mean this as an excuse, Emma, but your grandpa ... he said something would happen if I told you. I believed him. I ... My father had this inner ... power — so when he spoke, people listened. He never said anything frivolous or off-the-cuff. He always measured his words. I'm sure I loved him as a kid. But as I got older, I found his anger, his intensity, his need to control *everyone* — even people in town — frightening. Yet, I wanted to be near him. His contact with the bees was almost mystical. I took care of the bees when I was your age, but I was never really a ... a keeper, you know? At least not until this summer. It will be years before I know even half of what your grandpa MacFey knew. I should have listened."

"He told you to take me as your kid," I say. "You listened to him then. You did as you were told then."

"No, Emma, it was your dad and me who made that decision. Together. Nothing you can *do* or *say* or *feel* will change how we feel. Nothing." Tears roll down her cheeks.

"I'll see you later," I say through the terrible tightness in my throat. "I'm late."

Mom searches the clover field as if looking for answers to questions that wait to be asked. Then she sighs, a shuddering deep breath, and holds out a hand as if to touch me, but I grab my bike and put it between us.

In a small wobbly voice, she says, "You could work here, Emma. I'll find the money to pay you."

"I don't want to work here anymore."

I wheel my bike down the drive and don't look back, even though I know she'll stand on the same spot until I'm out of sight.

As I ride past Dad's field, I see him up on a ladder doing something with a length of wood. He waves to me but my hands are welded to the handlebars. He calls out something. I keep pedaling.

When I walk into Albert's kitchen, he's sitting at the table tying bundles of herbs with string. The room smells like Mom's pesto — crushed basil with a hint of licorice. He cries, "Well, look at you — like a pot of chives that hasn't been watered for a week, all droopy and pale green. Are you still suffering from that sunstroke? You know, *you* especially should be wary of the sun."

In a dull voice I say, "You don't know anything about me."

"I don't need to. Look at you — an everlasting flower, white on white. Can I help? One of my tonics to make you feel better?"

His cheery concern makes me snarl, "I don't need help from you — or *anyone*."

"Goodness, such *big* anger from one so small. What's happened? Did Tom upset you last night?"

That snaps me to attention. "How do you know I saw Tom last night?"

"Ummm, I think he told me he ran into you. You know, Emma, sometimes it helps to unload on someone you don't know that well — and I'm a good listener." He's trying to be nonchalant, but he won't look me in the eye.

I say firmly, "I don't know what Tom said to you, but it's no one's business but mine, okay? What fields are we weeding this morning? I brought a hat."

"Oh, Emma, Emma, it's not healthy to keep things in. I *know* this. And of course, you *must* be very careful who you talk to."

I press my lips together and narrow my eyes.

He shrugs. "Aaah well, I'm afraid I'm going to leave you for a bit. I have to find out where my stall is located on the market grounds. Janet should be here any minute. You can help her sort out some of the smaller potted herbs and price them, if you don't mind."

I do mind. A lot. "Doesn't your father need company? Maybe —"

"No! Don't on any account disturb him. He's resting. Had a bad night, you see. No, you help Janet."

He grabs his straw hat and sunglasses and darts from the room. A few minutes later the ancient truck grinds out of the yard. I sit in the silence of the kitchen. What did Tom say to him? Why do I have to work with that strange Janet person? Why is my life falling apart?

I jump to my feet, run upstairs and stand in front of the old man's closed door. I make a deal with myself. If he's sleeping, I'll go back downstairs. If he's awake, I'll convince him to play Fidchell. I turn the handle. The room is dim, the curtains closed except for a single strip of pale light that slides across the Turkish rug and strikes a pair of brown leather boots scrolled with swirling designs — boots that move swiftly into the shadows. I release the handle and stand very still, not breathing.

"Mr. Maxim?" I whisper into the silence.

His deep growl comes from the shadows to the right of the door. "Please go away, Sparrow. I'm resting."

"I — I thought maybe we could play Fidchell."

"Thank you, no," the voice says. "I don't want to be disturbed. Close the door as you go."

I lean in and catch the doorknob, and out of the corner of my eye, I see a short dark figure dressed in brown slip into the folds of the curtains that hang against the far wall.

My scalp prickles. It's Fergus, the man from the field last night. When I was sleepwalking. But I'm not sleeping now. Am I?

"Are you okay, Mr. Maxim?" I ask in a high squeak.

"Couldn't be better. Just a tad weary. Albert will not be happy to know you disobeyed him," Poppy's voice rumbles. "Best to say nothing about coming up here. Shut the door, Sparrow."

My legs are wobbly, but I manage to make it most of the way down the stairs, when I hear voices arguing below. I sink down on to the step, caught between two places I dare not go.

"You said you'd keep him immobile between the daystar and gloaming and now I find out you've taken the cunning off him altogether?" Tom Krift growls. "He says he's going to watch Sweeney's progress himself? Watching the Sweeneys is *my* job. The cunning was there to protect Fergus at his vulnerable times. He'll be at risk now. What were you *thinking?*"

Janet's voice spits back, "Don't you question me! *I'm* the Druvid. *He's* the Sover-reign. *You're* merely the *Watcher*. Soon we'll take the child and use the circle gate. He needs to be mobile at all times."

"And what about the gate? Sweeney's constantly in my way. Now Fergus will come at all hours and harass me. If your magic isn't strong enough to keep the portal from being breached — if Huw breaks your code —"

Janet snarls. "Huw will not break this one so easily. You say the gate is almost ready now. You keep the child's Watcher under your eye: I'll keep Fergus under mine."

Their angry voices are cut off when a door closes in the distance. My head whirls with questions and the echoes of their voices. *Watching the Sweeneys is* my *job.* Tom is watching all of us — even Dad. Why? And then he said, *What about the gate? Sweeney's constantly in my way.* What is he doing at Dad's henge? And Janet. *I'm the Druvid.* Druvid ... wasn't that what Queen Rhona called Huw? And Janet also named both Fergus and Huw. Most worrying was, *Soon we'll take the child and use the circle gate.*

This child they keep talking about. I know now for sure.

It's me.

24

I pedal furiously down the drive, the old bike rattling loudly. When I reach the gate and look back, I'm surprised no one is following me.

"This is crazy," I mutter. "Completely nuts."

If I go to the farm I'll have to face Mom. If I go to the henge I'll have Dad to contend with. As I approach his field, I get off the bike and walk it into the ditch. A line of mucky water runs along the bottom, but the grass and weeds have been flattened by the storm, so it's easy to walk beside it without getting my feet wet.

Keeping my head down, I make it past Dad's field without being seen and hide the bike in the bushes beside the old gate. Instead of following the path, I cut directly through the wood until I come to the shaded riverbank.

I sit down under a tall silver willow. The Brokenhead is deeper here, the color of iced tea, the rocks below like submerged ice cubes. Dappling shadows scatter over a sparrow ruffling its feathers in the warm water at the edge of the river. Suddenly exhausted, I lean against the willow's trunk and try to breathe in the peaceful silence around me. My muscles relax. I close my heavy eyelids and fall into a dreamless sleep.

When I wake up, I'm curled on my side, my head resting on my folded arm. I sit up and check my watch. Eight o'clock. I've slept for hours and hours! The sun is slanting through the willows, shining on the water like warm oil.

My head feels clear. I take a deep breath. Maybe now I can decide what's real and what isn't. *I have to*. I have to try and sort out what's really happening to me.

I'll start with the Krifts. Tom and his mother, Janet — if she *is* his mother — moved to town a few months ago. Just around the time Albert and Poppy Maxim moved to their farm. Coincidence? No. From what Tom and Janet said, they've known the Maxims for a long time. So, really, there are two sets of new people that moved to a town where new people are never welcomed. Mom told me that no one had been able to buy local property in that area for years unless they were related to someone from town. So how have four strangers managed it? Albert even has a market stall when normally only third-and fourth-generation Bruid- ites are allowed one.

And why do Tom and his mother and the Maxims pretend they didn't know one another before moving to town, when clearly they did? And — I have to face it — why were Tom and Janet throwing around words like "Druvid," "Sover-reign" and "Watcher," and why did they name the very people I saw and heard in my dreams? I did *not* imagine that conversation in the kitchen this morning.

What does it all mean? What do these people want here? Who are they?

I shake my head. I have to be careful not to confuse my strange dreams with what is real. An inner voice answers back, *But those dreams are what's real.*

Think logically. Don't give in to the confusion and fear. What is Tom's part in all this? Is *he* the one who ties everything together? Two days ago, he shows up at Dad's field. Then he starts working for *both* Albert and Dad. Then he starts hanging around the barn pretending to look at owls. Why was he hiding in the field last night? Why did he ask me to tell him if anything went wrong with my family?

Why? Why? *Why?*

I twist my fingers into my hair to slow down my whirling thoughts, but even more questions fly at me. Why did Tom and Janet talk about keeping watch over Dad's henge? How could they possibly *use* it? Why was Fergus in the old man's room? Do they know each other? I twist my fingers tighter. Am I going crazy?

I stare across the narrow stream. Breathe deep. Stay calm. If I accept, just for the moment, that the dreams are *real*, then the man Fergus — not Tom — is at the center of it all.

What do I know about this man with the strange black eyes and scar? He was supposed to marry Queen Rhona, and they were going to join two big kingdoms together. Huw told the queen that if they had been able to do this, that would have made the game even more exciting — they could have expanded it into uncharted realms. What game do they keep going on about? It can't be just a board game like Fidchell.

Fergus promised Rhona that he would give an island kingdom to her brother, Keir, to keep him out of their hair. But instead of being grateful, Keir tried to hurt Fergus's sister, Branwen. To punish him, Fergus turned Keir into that sea-land monster and took back the gift of the island kingdom. And *then* Fergus went in search of the child — the real heir to Argadnel — a child he'd hidden away for its own safety.

Rhona and Huw intend to find this mysterious child and kill it before Fergus can return it to the island of Argadnel. But something is stopping them. Something called a cunning lock, which seals the portal from their world to this one — the one they call Eorthe.

I go over everything again and again as the sun drops behind the trees. If I'm simply having strange dreams, then my family and I have nothing to fear from these people. But what if the dreams are real?

Am I really the child? Do they want to kill me? If I am the child, how can my family be in danger? Why would Tom tell me to call him if they were threatened in any way? Why did he tell me to watch over them? Mom, Dad ... and Summer.

I don't want to say it. But there's only one answer. I'm not the child they're looking for.

It's Summer.

25

I burst through the back door to find the family packing boxes for the market. Summer is piling cellophane-wrapped honey cakes in a small carton. There's a rim of milk on her upper lip. The skin around her eyes is gray, her face thin and pale, making her look like a Victorian street urchin. I feel such a flood of fear and relief at seeing her that it hurts my heart.

Mom cries, "Where have you been, Emma? We've been so worried!"

"I worked late in the fields," I say.

"It's almost dark, Emma. I think a phone call was in order." Dad's voice is tight. "I drove around and didn't see you anywhere. Even tried the Maxims'. No one home. I know this has been hard on you, but even so — it was really thoughtless. We worry —"

I shout, "*You* worry! All I do is worry! I mean, look at Summer. She's sick. And Mom's got her working. You're so busy in that stupid circle you're banging together, you don't even notice us half the time!"

"That's not fair, Emmy!" Summer cries. "You're just being mean because you're still mad at us. And it's all my fault."

Dad looks shaken. "I'm sorry, Emma. I know you worry about us. You'll come and talk to us when you're ready, right? I was just concerned, that's all."

Rage, fear and panic twist inside me. I want to tell them they're in danger, but how can I? There's no proof. None. Albert Maxim, Tom Krift, Janet, Poppy Maxim — they haven't actually done anything. How can I tell my family that people from my dreams are coming from another time and place to kill Summer?

All three of them are watching me with worried frowns. Mom holds a jar of amber honey, Dad an empty cardboard box, Summer a wrapped honey cake. All so ordinary. So normal. I must be going crazy. No one is going to hurt Summer.

"I'm sorry, okay?" I mutter. "I'm — I'm tired. Going to bed."

I run out the door but Mom catches up to me.

"Emma — Emma!"

I wait, shoulders hunched.

She stands in front of me, blocking my way up. "You heard what your dad said? You will come to us when you need to talk?"

I shrug.

"Also ..." Mom hesitates, then blurts out, "... you won't go near the henge, will you?"

"What?" I thought she was about to go on and on about my fake adoption again. Where has *this* come from? "Why?"

"I don't know. I went there to see how your dad was making out — I hadn't seen it close up and — well, I didn't like the vibes I was getting off it. Maybe it comes from my father's warnings to stay away from that field, but ..."

Dad's voice drifts through the warm night air. "Letonia! Leave Emma alone. We agreed!"

"I know, I know! I'm coming!" Mom calls back before grabbing hold of my arm and whispering urgently, "I want you to promise me you won't go near Grandpa MacFey's field. Never mind why. I just feel it's important. Promise?"

"Okay, okay. And you'd better watch out for Summer," I hiss. "You won't leave her alone tonight, right? Not for one second."

Mom's grip tightens. "Emma, what's wrong?"

I almost laugh out loud. I want to say, "Oh, nothing much. Only that two groups of people from some other world are after Summer — one to make her a queen, the other to kill her. Don't you see, Letonia Sweeney? Your poor changeling Pithwitchen daughter Emma-Winter is losing her mind."

Mom shakes my arm. "What is it, Emma? Tell me!"

"You tell me," I throw back. "Is there something I *should* know?"

I hope she'll make sense of it all, but she only gives an embarrassed laugh and says, "No … no … look, I'm sorry, sweetie. You get some sleep, and we'll have a good time tomorrow at the market. Right?"

"Yeah … right."

After searching my face, she says, "I love you very much, Emma."

I watch her walk into the glow of the back door's light. I've never lied to Mom before this past week, and now that's all I seem to be doing. Yet, I have to let the madness lead me … to what, I don't know. When the screen door slaps shut, I stride quickly down the driveway toward Grandpa MacFey's wood.

26

The moon hangs like a circle of rice paper above the dark arch of willows guarding the entrance to the wood. If I go through there, will I end up in the twisted-tree maze — like the one I was caught in before, like the one on the Fidchell board?

I walk along the fence until I come to the edge of Dad's field. The air is clouded with midges, fireflies and the steeped heady fragrance of wild roses — the only sounds the faint peep of frogs and whir of crickets.

I climb the fence. From this distance the henge is silhouetted against the darkening sky, looking exactly like the one in Dad's sketchbook — utterly still, heavy and strangely secretive. He didn't say anything about finishing it today. But then he didn't have much of a chance to tell us, did he?

As I walk closer to the Plexiglas monoliths, the moon's glow drifts over rough Celtic symbols etched into the surface, many of them crescent and full moons.

"The moon is the lord of time," Dad told me when he was planning the circle, "and the symbol of endless life — of immortality." That's when he pointed at my strange birthmark and said, "I chose them because they've marked you in a special, almost magical way, too. Those little marks on your wrist have always reminded me of crescent moons. And you've always looked like you were a tiny moon goddess with your pale eyes and white hair."

That comment had made me look at the birthmark closely for the first time in years. I could see a vague outline that might be crescent moons but I'd smiled indulgently, thinking he was, as usual, way over the top. In the last few days the mark has definitely been changing shape, even altering colors — from pink to blue to green. Why?

Did my real mother have such a mark? I'll never know. I rub the stain on my wrist. I hate this reminder of the fearsome aloneness — the separation from the only family I've known, from the place where I know I've never really belonged, but want back desperately.

When I step inside the circle, a pallid light glances off the frosted surfaces, suddenly silvering them into a circle of wavering mirrors. And in those moonstruck looking glasses, I see something that stops my heart.

Slowly and deliberately, I lift one arm. Drop it. Lift it again. Who is that creature repeated in the misty mirrors over and over — the one imitating my actions — the one with the white hair fanned high about its narrow head and large ears, the face creamy white, the slanted eyes glinting darkly, a long cloak of dappled light swirling around it?

Is it me?

Mesmerized, I move toward one of the mirrors, but as I draw closer, the moonlight dissolves and I am *me* again — except my hair still floats around my head. I try to flatten it, but it sproings back up into a fan of white gold. A warm breath of air wafts around me and the fan drifts back into place.

I go to the exact center of the circle, expecting to see the hole where the lightning struck, but Dad has been busy here, too. He's put a Plexiglas tube into the hole. The tube is about as wide as my palm in diameter and a little higher than my waist. On top of it is a long wide slab of clear Plexiglas, etched with more rough designs. He said he was going to make such a table — he called it a socle. At each corner of the socle is a carved wooden support, the clear strawlike tube of plastic a fifth brace in the middle. Leaning over the slab of plastic, I see that he's cut a perfect circle in it, leaving the mouth of the tube exposed.

I hold my hand over it. A cold steady breeze rises out of the opening with a faint whistling sound. The henge stones surround me like enormous blocks of smoky ice.

Earlier today Tom asked Janet if her magic was strong enough to keep the portal from being breached. What did he mean? If Dad's henge is the portal, the door between this world and Huw and Rhona's, maybe ... just maybe ...

I dig in my pocket for my piece of amethyst. The bigger chunk had turned a blazing red color just before Tom grabbed it last night. Did the amethyst have some sort of magical power? Will the same thing happen if I put mine over the hole?

The crystal is cold and sharp in my clenched hand. I place it over the opening of the Plexiglas tube, resting its pointed tips on the tabletop. Then I step back.

Of course, nothing happens. My giggle is high and shrill in the still air. Why should I be surprised? Dad's an artist, not a Druvid. His plans came from the Internet, for crying out loud. Everyone knows you can't rely on anything you find there. He couldn't possibly have created something with magical powers. *Magic? Druvids? Hey, now I'm even crazier than Dad.*

Suddenly the earth heaves under my feet. I hear a faint click nearby. My little crystal lifts slowly into the air above the tube's opening. It turns dark yellow, then glows red. I dash across the circle toward the oak just as a deep growling cough echoes through the henge and a spear of hot white light drives straight up from the table.

It illuminates the entire field for one blinding moment before spreading across the sky into the glowing branches of a giant tree. The branches splinter into a million tiny lights that zoom over the fields like a magical swarm of bees. The stem of light drops back into the tube with a deep rushing moan.

Is it over? I'm about to step out from behind the oak when a tight mass of flashing blue lights flits away from the socle, passes right through one of Dad's Plexiglas stones and vanishes. I remember to take a breath, but it catches in my throat when a broad amorphous shape edged in a faint glitter of light slides off the table and shudders along the inside of the circle as if searching for a way out. It passes by one of the Plexiglas mirrors and the plastic wrinkles and twists, then settles back to normal as the thing moves toward the oak. Toward me.

My feet pound the hard ground, aiming for the fence, four words echoing in my head over and over — *what have I done, what have I done, what have I done?* I jump the fence, my feet barely skimming the earth when I land on the other side, fierce and frightened, blood roaring in my ears. I race down the driveway to the house and collapse on the back steps, gasping for air. I realize my mistake — I hadn't dared to look back. What if that thing followed me? I've led it to my family. I'm on my feet again in a flash.

I reach the road, cross it, slide into the ditch and edge my way back to the fence surrounding Dad's field. That's when I spot the thing again. The moon's faint glow catches it in a filmy web of light as it slips up from the ditch onto the road. I can see right through it, the highway twisting and rippling as it moves away from the farm, toward town.

I run to the house, open the back door and both curse and bless Dad for not locking it. I click the dead bolt shut and stand in the dark kitchen trying to decide what to do, then creep past piles of cardboard honey boxes and up the stairs. Dad's snoring echoes down the hall. I ease into Summer's room on tiptoes. Every detail stands out clearly — the collection of Barbie dolls lined up along the low bookshelf, a pair of pale socks lying in a crumpled heap at the side of the bed. I've always been able to see really well in the dark but tonight it's as if there are tiny flashlights inside my eyes bathing everything in clarity. The room is hot and Summer is sprawled across the bed on her back, covers flowing onto the floor. She's wearing her favorite Bat Girl shortie pajamas. Her thin white legs and knobby knees make my chest contract with pain.

I have to protect her.

27

Every now and again I creep into Summer's room to check on her, then go downstairs to walk from window to window, staring out at the night. Once, from the living room window, I think I see the owl flying to the barn, but can't be sure, because it goes by so swiftly. The rest of the time, I sit at the top of the stairs, eyes wide, ears alert. Before dawn, I pack the truck, which Dad had parked close to the back door before he went to bed.

By the time my parents are stirring, I've loaded everything, ticking items off the list Mom left on the table. She wanders in looking exhausted and stares around at the gleaming kitchen. Slices of toast are stacked on a warm plate, a pot of tea steams on the table.

"Hey, where are all the boxes?" she asks.

"In the truck."

"Oh my," she says in a wobbly voice. "This is wonderful, Emma! I was dreading all the work this morning. Thank you, sweetheart." She hugs me.

"I have to go into town for a few minutes before I go to the market," I say, gently removing her arms.

"Why? Can't you be with us? Are you helping Albert or something?"

"No. He has two others to help him. But I promised to run a couple of errands for his father. In town."

"Oh?"

"Some books from the used bookstore and a few things — at the hardware store." It's easy to lie when you've planned it all night. "I thought I'd take Summer with me."

"Mmm, I don't know, Emma. There are weird electropulsations today that I can't pin down and — well, I'd rather both of you were with Dad and me."

"We won't be long."

Summer wanders into the kitchen, looking more fragile than yesterday — smaller, thinner — as if she's slowly fading away.

"Take me where?" she asks, yawning.

"Sweetie, I don't think you should go anywhere. You don't look up to it!" Mom exclaims.

"Oh, Mommy, please? I'll be better after breakfast." She grabs some toast. "See? I'm eating. I've got my inhaler. Please don't make me stay home! I promised Lacey!"

"Well …," Mom says. "I guess I could set up a makeshift bed in the tent for when you need it. But I don't know about you doing errands with Emma."

Summer looks pleased. "Where are we going, Emmy?"

"Into town," I say, then turn to Mom. "You and Dad will be busy setting up, and she'll just get in the way. We can take our time, and slowly walk back to the market, and be there when you need us — it's not far."

"Well ...," she says reluctantly. "I guess so."

Dad walks in, bewildered, then peers out the back door. "Hey! The truck's loaded."

"Emma did it," Mom says. "Wasn't that sweet of her?"

"I want to get going this morning, that's all," I say. "It's no big deal."

"It is to us. Thanks, Emma." Dad runs his hand over my head. Suddenly I want to grab hold of that rough hand and tell him everything that's happening, but how can I? It would sound ... even Dad, for all his openness to strange ideas, wouldn't believe this one. It's crazier than anything he could imagine. No, I have to do this on my own. Or maybe, with luck, I can get one other person's help. If I can trust him.

Dad grabs a pile of toast and pours a mug of tea. "By the way, tired or not, we're having a family meeting tonight. We *all* need to talk."

He bangs out through the door. Summer follows. I start after them, but Mom says, "Emma?"

I look at the floor. I can't let her see my fear.

"What's worrying you, Emma? Is it, you know … us?"

I clear my throat. "Why didn't you want me to go near the henge last night? It can't just be because of a vague feeling."

Startled, she says, "Well … I've thought about it, and I really think it has to do with how my dad felt and acted about that dumb field. Isn't that silly? I'm an adult now, not the little kid who didn't want to make my dad mad at me. But when I looked at it on my way home from the market grounds yesterday, it made me remember something. A long time ago, when I was about twelve or thirteen, some kids from town got into the field and knocked down all my dad's neatly piled cairns."

"Cairns?"

"Just piles of stone he'd dug out of the ground. He'd arranged them in a big circle. Lots of farmers have piles of rocks here and there — rocks that were in the way of their planting and stuff. I guess your grandpa liked the symmetry of the circle. He liked lining up his hives just so, too. He always wanted … order. Anyway, these kids started throwing the rocks around and got the cows into a frenzy. One cow was badly injured. And they even knocked over some of the hives in that far field behind the river. Dad was furious — went straight into town. The next day at school, three boys were really mad at me because they'd been given a good thrashing by their fathers. They couldn't get mad at Dad so they took it out on me. One of them was Lacey's father, Duncan MacIvor. We never got along after that. It was like he had a grudge against my dad or something."

"But why warn *me* against the field? Dad's there every day."

"I told you it was silly. It goes back to something my dad said the night the boys were caught. I heard him tell my mother that no one was allowed to go into the field because ... what was it exactly? ... oh yes, he said they had to stay away from the circle gate — even though it had been locked for years and years."

"Circle gate?"

"I could never figure out what he was talking about. There was no round gate that I knew of. People in town used to call him the Keeper. I guess because he kept bees — but to me it was almost as if he was keeping watch over that field." She shivers. "I asked my mother a few times, but she wouldn't talk about it. It's ridiculous, but as soon as your dad started building that thing in the field, I was sorry I'd ever mentioned Bruide Henge."

"Did you go to that field when you were a kid to look for this circle gate he talked about?"

Mom shakes her head. "I helped him with the bees, but he looked after the cows and the field himself. He said when I was eighteen I could take over from him — that he'd pass on a great honor to me when the time was right. But I didn't stick around to find out what this *honor* stuff was. I just took Mom's money and split for college. I didn't want to spend my life looking after the farm just because he said so." She laughs. "But look — he was right!"

"Did he mean for you to take over the bee farm? Or did he mean something else?" I ask.

"Like what?"

"Like something he had hidden in the field?"

"Hidden in the field?" Mom stares at me.

I don't answer. Dad's honking the horn outside and I have to ask something even more important. "When Summer was born, did anything strange happen to her — to you?"

Mom gapes at me.

I grab her arm. "I know it was hard to tell me how I was born, but I have to know — is Summer your *real* daughter. Please, *please* don't lie."

The blood drains from Mom's face. "Of course she's our real child. Yes, yes, she is. They said she was."

"Who said?"

"The midwife ... and my father. I have to admit that as time drew closer to Summer's birth, I started remembering how upset I was over the last ... baby, and I got more and more worried ... more frightened. Then, to my horror, Summer came two weeks early, before your dad and I were able to get near the hospital. In fact, Dennis was in Winnipeg looking for a place for us to stay. I don't remember much about the birth, I was so scared. But … yes, sweetheart, she's our child."

"Are you *sure?*" I want to believe her so much.

She sighs and puts her hand on my shoulder. "Yes, Emma. I know how hard this has been on you. But she is my child. And although you're not my birth child, you *are* my daughter, too."

"Why did you cry all the time after she was born?"

"Did I? I don't remember. I was probably crying from happiness." She's lying. She remembers.

"Then why did it make *me* feel so sad?"

The truck horn blares insistently.

"Mom," I say urgently, "after Summer was born I heard Grandpa MacFey and that midwife talking. He told her she'd done the right thing, that his grandchild would go to a better place. He talked about being part of something really big and important. And when he spotted me listening, he told her that she'd done the right thing with me, too. And that he'd watch over you and your family."

Mom's eyes blink rapidly, as if she can't take in what I'm saying. "You heard Ina MacIvor and my father talking about … you and Summer? What did she say to him?"

"She said something about the old ways being hard. That's all I remember. Except she seemed really upset."

"Ina? She wasn't much older than me. How could she know about the old ways? You mustn't have heard properly. You were a little kid." With shaking hands, she grabs a handful of leaflets off the table. "We really need to talk ... when we have more time, Emma. Maybe see a counselor or something —"

But I don't wait to hear any more. I run outside, climb onto the back of the truck and sit on a pile of burlap that's part of the stall decoration. Summer's already sitting on a row of boxes, taking small bites from her piece of toast, her skinny legs jiggling with anticipation of the day ahead. Mom is so sure Summer is her real child. She must know. Maybe I'm wrong about the danger we're in. I try to relax, but my muscles are stiff as concrete.

Mom climbs in beside Dad after giving me a troubled look. As the truck bumps up onto the highway, my stomach squeezes into a double knot. We'll soon be passing Dad's henge. I won't look. I'll concentrate on the warmth of the sun on my back, the soft breeze that carries the sweet smell of purple clover, the bees that float above the heavy blossoms in the field.

I wish myself back before any of this happened. Everything made sense then. Nothing makes sense anymore. Was last night another sleepwalking dream? Was any of it real? Is *this* real — the fields, the sun, the growling engine of the truck, Summer's hair blowing around her thin eager face? Is Summer really Mom and Dad's child, or was she brought to the farm — like me? If so, what happened to the baby Mom gave birth to that day? Grandpa MacFey said she'd gone to a better place. Heaven? Did she die? Summer catches my eye and grins, her small nose wrinkling with happiness. I look away to keep from crying.

We pass the wood and soon the wide clearing of Dad's field comes into view. I force myself not to look. But, naturally, Dad has to stop the truck, get out and show off. He sweeps his arm through the air and cries, "Take a gander at that! Look at how the sun's hitting it! Looks like real stone!"

"Gee, Dad, it's absolutely amazing," breathes Summer. "Hey, can I have my birthday party in it next month?"

"Don't see why not," he says. "Odd, you know, it looks more finished than it actually is. I still have quite a few things to do. I haven't even made the center socle yet — I might use treated wood for that."

But the socle was there last night. I placed the crystal piece on it and then ... my mind veers away from ... after that.

Dad's voice cuts through my tangled thoughts, "... call the press when it's finished and we'll have a party in the circle. A real pagan celebration. Won't that be great? Leto, what do you think? Isn't it *absolutely amazing?*"

Mom stands by the truck, staring at Bruide Henge.

"Isn't it absolutely amazing, Mom? Isn't it?" Summer cries.

Mom doesn't move. I can tell — she feels it, too. She knows something's wrong. I can't help it — I follow her gaze. The henge looks just like it did last night. The Plexiglas looked like stones then, too. I shiver, remembering the pale other-worldly creature repeated in the silvery mirrors in the circle, the bizarre clump of blue lights and the strange shapeless thing that slithered out of the circle. Where are they now? Locked inside my dream, inside my crazy head?

Mom climbs back into the truck and slams the door.

"Okay, kids, let's go," Dad says. "Mom's anxious to get the stall set up."

I look through the back window of the truck at my mother's stiff neck and shoulders. She's definitely afraid of something. And this time I know I'm not imagining it.

28

Bruide has one main street with a gas station, a small supermarket, a hardware store, a chip shop, an ice-cream parlor, a small bookstore and a thrift shop. Leading off it are a handful of tree-lined roads with a scattering of old houses behind high bushes.

Dad parks the truck so its nose is aimed at the curb, like everyone else in town does. Summer and I hop down from the flatbed.

Dad peers out the truck window at the empty street. "Wow, a market ghost town, huh? Mom says you're going to buy something at the bookstore for Mr. Maxim. Doesn't look open."

I shake my head and boldly fib once more. "It will be. I called yesterday."

Mom, a troubled frown creasing her forehead, says, "Emma ... it's not far, but ... you won't be long, will you?"

"No, we'll be there soon," I assure her, not having any idea if that's a lie.

Dad revs the engine. "See you in a bit. Call the market office if you need a lift. They'll page us."

I nod and the truck makes a U-turn and drives off, Mom looking through the back window with that anxious look still streaked across her face. I stare after her until the truck disappears down a side street toward the old highway and the market grounds.

"Hey, Emma," Summer calls, "let's go!" She starts toward the bookstore.

"Not that way. I want to go here first," I say, pointing to MacIvor's ice-cream shop.

Summer brightens immediately. "Maybe Lacey hasn't left yet. I can get a ride with them."

"No! Stay with me. It's important." I say it so fiercely Summer gapes at me.

"Okay, okay. Jeez, no big deal. Why do you want to go here anyway?"

"Uh — Mr. Maxim wants me to find out if they sell ginger ice cream."

"Yuck."

In the front window of the shop is a sign that reads, "Closed for market day. Come and visit us at our green and yellow stall." Maybe I'm too late. But when we walk around the back of the building, Lacey's dad is filling a freezer van with frosted plastic tubs. He's a small dark man with lots of black hair on his arms and almost none on his head. So this is the man who made my grandfather so angry years ago. Was he *still* messing around in the field — with Dad's henge? Maybe he's the one who wrote the note. Wait, of course! His wife is Ina MacIvor, the midwife who'd taken me from my real mother and given me to Mom. And who was also at Summer's birth.

He looks up and spots Summer. "Lacey's upstairs. Tell her to get a move on or I'm goin' without her," he growls.

Summer runs into the shop. Mr. MacIvor slams the back panels of the van shut, eyes me up and down, and says, "You're the other Sweeney kid, right?"

"Yes." I decide to start with something simple. "Do you know where Tom Krift lives?"

"Down Orkney Road. Got a trailer. Can't miss it."

"Thanks. And could you tell me something else?"

"Yeah? What's that?" He straightens up and looks at me through narrowed eyes.

"Your son ... well ... he said you and your wife called me something — a Pithwitchen. Your wife knew my birth mother."

"I don't know nothin' about where you come from, kid," he says, gruffly.

"You don't know who my real mother is?"

"No idea. Ignore my kid. He's talkin' rubbish as usual."

"Can I talk to Mrs. MacIvor?"

"Already gone to the market. And you'll not get nothin' outta her, neither."

"Maybe she'd talk to me," I say.

"She never talks about her time as a midwife. Stopped doin' that nine years back. She keeps herself to herself now. Like everyone else in this town."

"You knew my grandpa," I say.

"Everyone knew Ewan MacFey," he sneers.

"Do you know why he was known as the Keeper? Or why he had cairns of stones in his field that he called the circle gate?"

Mr. MacIvor's face and neck flush an ugly red. He stomps toward the back of his shop. "That's a load of crap. I gotta lot of work to do. I'm already late for the market. Lacey! Get out here right this minute."

The two girls appear, each carrying a triple-scoop ice cream. Lacey licks hers with gusto, but Summer holds hers to one side as if the smell bothers her.

Something makes me say quietly to the man, "Do you know who sent my parents a note warning them that the henge my dad's building in my grandpa's field might be cursed? The note also talked about a child being the cause of something. Did you send it? I need to know who the child —"

"No!" He shouts. The two girls stare goggle-eyed at him. I flinch but stand my ground.

"Did you send it?" I repeat. "Did you also mess around in the field?"

"What're you going on about! Get outta here!" Mr. MacIvor shouts, waving his arms in the air. "You're a troublemaker, like your ma. She was always a pain, even when we was kids. She came here bothering me the other night. I'll tell you the same thing I told her. I don't know nothin' about you or your sister and I don't care to, neither! Lacey, get in the truck. Now!"

Lacey runs for the van, calling over her shoulder, "See you there, Summer!"

Mr. MacIvor guns the engine and roars away down the lane.

"Jeez, what was that all about?" Two bright red spots are glowing on Summer's cheeks. "What did you say to him, Emmy?"

I can't answer. There's something in the air — perhaps a sound I've barely registered, perhaps a smell, I'm not sure, but I take Summer's hand and creep along the side of the building, my eyes taking in every piece of grass on the path and fleck of paint on the walls. Ordering her to stay behind me, I glance around the corner of the shop to make sure everything is clear.

It isn't.

29

I pull Summer back against the shop's stucco wall.

"Emmy, what —" she says, but I shush her with one hand over her mouth.

"Don't move, don't speak. Danger," I whisper urgently.

I peer once more around the corner of the wall. I can't see the man's face, but he's tall and bone-thin, wearing jeans, a shimmery blue T-shirt and a lot of heavy silver jewelry around his neck. He has smooth gray hair pulled into a loose braid that hangs down his back. His wrists are encrusted with chunky silver bracelets, his upper arms covered in pale blue tattoos. Every hair on my head prickles with alarm.

He turns slowly, his gaze taking in everything. That's when I see the swirling blue design on the left side of his face.

Huw.

His gaze lands on the sign in the ice-cream shop window. I pull back quickly, wish us invisible and feel us sink into the rough stucco wall. We wait for what seems like hours, then to my horror he appears right in my line of vision. His gaze sweeps the entire street including our hiding place. I tighten my hand over Summer's mouth. His gaze moves on, like a searchlight. Why doesn't he see us? I sag with relief when he goes back the way he came. I wait a few seconds, then brave a quick look. He's walking quickly away from us down the street. He's not dragging that strange lighted echo of himself around, but there's a shimmering glob of something sliding right behind him, distorting his legs like flowing water. Does he know it's there?

I pull back again and wait. Summer tugs on my hand impatiently. Cautiously, I take another peek. He's gone, but I'm scared Summer will speak in her shrill little voice and bring him back.

I whisper, "Don't say a word, Summer. Not ... one ... sound."

Summer, wide-eyed, nods. I release my hand just as the sound of an engine rumbles down the street. Mr. MacIvor's van appears at the lane between the two buildings where we're standing. I step from the shadow.

"Hey! You still here?" he snarls out his window. "Beat it. I don't want you hangin' around my place."

"Daddeee! Pleeease! It's so embarrassing!" comes an anguished cry from the passenger's seat.

"Did you pass a tall man with blue tattoos on the street just now?" I demand.

Mr. MacIvor growls, "Listen, kid, I'm goin' to tell your parents you've been hasslin' me, talking garbage and accusing me of stuff I had nothin' to do with. I told your mom she shoulda never brought you two back here. All that crap ended when your bully of a grandpa died. And good riddance, I say. Those old stories — them Blue Celtoi and all those others — ain't true. Everyone knows that. Your dad's playin' with fire — he's cursin' that field —"

"So it *was* you who wrote that note," I say. "Why can't you tell me —?"

He swears loudly, puts the truck into gear and drives off with a squeal of tires, Lacey wailing in dismay.

"Man, has he gone weird or what?" Summer says. "He's always loud, but really nice. What's wrong with him?"

I'm hardly listening. The Blue Celtoi? Wasn't that the tribe Rhona said Huw belonged to? Do other people in town know about them?

I've got to find Tom. I grab Summer's hand and run until I come to a heavily treed gravel lane called Orkney Road. Checking that Huw isn't in sight, I drag Summer down it.

30

"Emma ... please ... I can't ..."

I yank Summer's arm and she stumbles and falls. "I ... want to run — but — I — can't —seem to — breathe ...," she whimpers. She's still holding her cone, but the ice cream is long gone and all that remains is a mangled bit of sugar cone.

I take the soggy remains out of her hand. I know I've pushed her too hard, but it's dangerous to stop. I crouch down with my back to her, wind my arms around her bony knees and lift. Her thin arms wrap around my neck. I'm shocked at how light she is. It can't be far to Tom's trailer. That awful Mr. MacIvor said I couldn't miss it.

We pass what seems like miles of dense bush and poplar trees until finally we come to a clearing where I spot a small green trailer, almost hidden by yellow willows.

I knock on the door and fight down panic when no one answers. "Oh god, please be here," I whisper.

What did he say to me? *Think of me — I mean really think about me.* I close my eyes and imagine his black hair, his thick body, his warm ugly face. I jump when a voice behind me says, "I've been searching for you everywhere. You're good at closing yourself off. I'm impressed."

"Tom," I say. "There's a man — I saw him —"

"I know. He's here."

"You know about him?"

"I decided not to tell the others. Not yet. I'll be in big trouble — but we're safe for a while." He examines Summer's face. "She's fading. It was inevitable."

"What's inevitable? What do you mean *fading?*"

Tom says, "I've got something I can give her until we decide what to do."

He takes Summer from me as if she's a feather, snaps open the door and carries her down a short hall.

"Doesn't your mother live with you?" I ask, for there's no sign of anything that might belong to Janet Krift.

Tom gently lays Summer down on a narrow bed.

"She's got her own place," he says. "We don't always get along."

The old trailer has been gutted and rebuilt inside. Everything is painted white except the floor, which is a hard shiny green. Other than the bed, there are only two chairs and a small white table.

Tom touches part of the wall and a small alcove opens up. Inside are a number of pale green bottles. He takes one down, opens it and turns it upside down on one fingertip. Then he touches a spot under each of Summer's earlobes as if he's applying perfume. Summer opens her eyes wide. A warm blush touches her ashen cheeks.

"Wow," she breathes. Then she closes her eyes, curls up and goes to sleep.

"What did you give her?" I demand.

"It can only be used once if it's not to harm her — she's too weak for more. Puts her into a kind of hibernation. It would be better if she was awake and stronger, but we'll just have to carry her."

"What if she wakes up? Why can't you use it again? Carry her where?"

"Sit down, Emma." Tom pulls a chair close and sits across from me, our knees touching.

"I have so many questions, Tom."

"Ask away."

I take a deep breath. "Who am I?"

"You're a Watcher, like me."

"A *Watcher*?"

"Yes. Our tribe is known as the Hidden Ones. We range through many worlds." He looks over at Summer. "She's not one of us."

My skin feels icy cold. I give a choked little laugh. "Tribe? Watcher? Hidden Ones? You're crazy, aren't you? I'm crazy, too. We're not living in the real world anymore, are we? Look, I'm adopted. She isn't. Summer's important because she belongs to my parents. I don't know ... where I belong." I try to keep the panic from my voice.

He shakes his head. "You don't belong to the Sweeneys, Emma, that's true. But neither does Summer."

31

"Oh, poor Mom, poor Dad." I can hardly breathe.

"I'm sorry."

I gulp hard. "But where *do* I come from? Where does *Summer* come from?"

"You were — uh — born in a secret place whose name I can't say. Summer is from an island world called Argadnel."

"I had some strange dreams. Two people called Rhona and Huw were talking about Argadnel. It was supposed to be given to someone called Keir, but he made someone called Fergus angry, and Fergus took it away from him. I heard them first when I was in a cave and then later on I ended up in a room that was part of Queen Rhona's home. And that time in the field I thought I saw Fergus and his sister — but I was *dreaming*."

Tom raises his eyebrows. "You heard Huw and the queen of Fomorii actually talking?"

"Yes. And I saw them, too. And I just saw Huw again. Here. In Bruide. Please, Tom — they were all dreams, right? Some sort of weird daydreams? You didn't lie to me that night … did you?"

He stares at me, his dark eyes intense. "No. They weren't daydreams. When you were in Sweeney's field two nights ago, you really did see Fergus and the others. I'm sorry I had to lie to you. That's why I told you to be careful that night. But I had no idea that you'd actually traveled to the border cave and then to Fomorii — but then …" He shrugs. "… why not? You're a Watcher. Even so, hitting the target, Rhona's base, is phenomenal. Your instincts must be highly tuned."

"Traveled?" I clutch his arm. "Not dreamed it? But actually traveled? Is that why it was so … real? When I was in the cave I saw two scenes — a big sea and another that was all jungly trees and vines that tried to grab me. The two places seemed to be separated by an invisible … wall and —" I'm talking so fast, I lose my breath.

Tom puts his hand over mine. "You saw the border between Rhona's undersea world of Fomorii and Fergus's homeland of Cleave. Very few beings can actually see the borderlands at the same time — you were looking through a kind of time warp. It's —"

I interrupt, breathlessly. "You say I'm a Watcher. Rhona asked Huw why they didn't get one of the Hidden Tribe — a Watcher — to go ahead of them to Eorthe. She said that Watchers can slide from world to world without using portals."

Tom nods.

I continue, "And Huw said that he was sure that even a Watcher couldn't go through Mathus's cunning lock. So how could *I?*"

Tom smiles and touches the center of my forehead with the tip of his finger. "Your Source must have been truly gifted. That's probably why they chose you to watch over the child. But you'll have to be trained to use your gift, or you could accidentally slide into one of a dozen different worlds without knowing how or when it's going to happen. You could really get yourself into serious trouble."

Half of me listens to him and accepts what he's saying, the other half is shrieking, *This is crazy! He's lying! Don't listen. Take Summer. Get away from him!*

But instead of bolting, I ask, "My Source?"

He looks uncomfortable. "The one who gave you life."

"My mother?"

He shrugs. "If you like."

"But who is she?"

"I was told by Fergus that your Source is no longer."

"You mean dead?" I whisper.

"I suppose you would call it that."

"And my father?"

"I don't know about fathers," he says stiffly. "Emma … you'll never find out. I don't know my

Source. We're taught never to ask. Watchers are reared differently than — than other beings." He slides the copper bracelet off his left wrist and shows me a large birthmark. It's two starlike shapes in the middle of a full moon.

I take a deep breath. "So you have one, too."

He nods. "It's the brand of a Watcher."

"And we don't … come from Earth, is that what you're saying? We come from where — another planet, like little green aliens?" I laugh, a dry bitter sound in the quiet room.

"Not other planets — other *worlds*," he says, "in many different planes of existence. Most of the tribes on these worlds are too volatile to ever fuse into one people. Their greatest excitement, like the tribes here on your Earth, is to battle one another — to conquer, to gain, to take. All Players through the different worlds call it by one name — the Game."

"By the Game, do you mean war?"

"Sometimes. It depends on the players and their preferences. Some choose a goal and then the opponents race to get to it first. There's usually land, wealth, even other players as the prize."

"They use *people* as prizes?"

"One opponent may bet fifteen thousand of his or her 'people' against a piece of coveted land, for instance. But, Emma, it doesn't matter what material stuff is at stake, what really matters is *winning*. It's the control, the power they get from winning that makes them need more. In Game mode, they're ruthless — they'll do anything to win. All of the other stuff is just a symbol of winning."

"Poppy Maxim said the same thing about winning. But he meant a board game called Fidchell."

Tom gives me a wry smile. "Oh, did he?"

"What happens when a game is over?"

"The players rest awhile, play, have fun — and then they set up another game — with different players — or a rematch with even higher stakes."

"And Fergus and Queen Rhona are involved in a game right now?"

"Yes. But this time it's more complicated because they had planned an alliance through a wedlock match. This happens sometimes when two key players decide to join forces. Passions run pretty high in the Game. Fergus and Rhona were very attracted to each other. It looked like a good union."

"And Keir messed it up."

"Completely. He demanded to marry Branwen, Fergus's sister, but she just laughed at him. He was so enraged he attacked her one night, tried to kill her. Fergus ordered Rhona to punish her brother. When she refused, he had Mathus put a beast cunning on Keir, broke off his plans with Rhona, challenged her to try and stop him, and for revenge went off to collect the legitimate heir to the throne of Argadnel. In other words, he spun a game into life out of sheer fury. A bad way to end an alliance and an even worse way to start a game."

"And now Rhona and Huw have tracked him here."

"Huw is no fool. He's found the old portal, and broken the cunning lock, and he'll take the child if he can."

"Summer?" My mouth goes dry with fear.

Tom nods again. "We've been trying to rebuild the portal from this side. Your dad's design was actually quite effective, but I had to make some significant changes. The old Keeper's circle — your grand-da's — was much simpler, and he would have been able to guide us through its preparation. We had no idea how powerful its energy was. I guess when the old Keeper died, it lost its fine-tuning. I gave it one small tweak one day and *blam!* — all that stored up electricity set off that hailstorm. But now it's ready to go."

"Ready to go?"

"I did the final alterations before sun-up, but I'm sure Huw was already here by then, which is good, because he doesn't know it's ready for a return path. Neither does Fergus. So you and I have a slight advantage, Emma. We can get Summer to safety. If we really move."

"They can't be allowed to take her. They can't!"

"I won't let them. I promise." He clears his throat. "But, Emma, you do know she must still go to Argadnel."

"Can't you make it so she can stay here?" I beg.

Gently Tom says, "If we don't get her back to her native world, Emma, she'll die."

"You keep saying *we*. Does that mean I can go with you — with her?"

"Yes. But we haven't much time, Emma. You can see she's fading quickly in this atmosphere. Fergus knew he'd have to come and get her when she reached this age, as he couldn't risk her death." He grimaces. "Having control over any potential sover-reign is important in the Game. And in this case, Summer was to become a pawn in his competition with Rhona. The Game is in the air they breathe — they are never happier than when in the middle of it."

"I still can't believe that Summer is the *child* they kept talking about."

"One of her own kinsmen — her uncle — won a game against her family. He killed them and made himself king. Fergus was secretly able to remove the newborn before the uncle could lay his hands on her. He needed a good hiding place, so he chose an old, almost forgotten world — Eorthe. Now the uncle is dead and it's possible for Fergus to give the people their rightful heir back — if he *chooses* to, that is."

"But Fergus was planning to give Argadnel to Keir, wasn't he?" I say indignantly, "because that suited his purpose *then*. And maybe Summer *wouldn't* have been brought to her homeland! She could just as easily have been left here to die. Fergus is almost as bad as her uncle!"

Tom shrugs. "You must understand, Emma — Fergus, Rhona, all of them — are not honorable beings. They don't behave the way *you* think people of honor should act. They're merciless and cold-blooded and when it comes to the Game, admit no limits. But they do have their own rules of honor. If Keir had behaved himself — he would have been given Argadnel — Summer would probably have become part of Fergus's household, cared for as if she were his child — schooled, taught the Ways — never knowing who she really was. Unless Keir got him angry again, and then the child could be used to foil Keir.

"You see, Emma, the people of Argadnel don't know their little queen is safe yet. But when they do — if I'm able to take her back before Fergus or Huw can get hold of her — her tribe will fight to the death to keep her. It's her only chance for safety."

"Why are you helping me, Tom?" I ask. "You could just take her to Fergus. He *claims* he's taking her to the island."

He reddens slightly. "Because Fergus will use her to control Argadnel. She'd be queen in name only. He could just as easily trade her off in a game if he saw it would be to his advantage. Besides, he'd never let you anywhere near her. He knows your loyalty and your potential skills. He'd never trust you. I know you have to be with her. She will always be vulnerable — and controllable — without you watching over her. She has to go back now."

"But, Tom, this will kill my parents! I love them too much to do this to them!" I am surprised at my own words. It's true. *I do love them.* How can I allow Summer to be taken away? "I can't do it to them, Tom. I can't."

He chews his bottom lip. "This — love — it's an attachment I know little of."

"It means you'd do *anything* for the other person — even die for them — to protect them *always*."

"Then you must do this for Summer, because you love her," he says softly.

"Mom and Dad won't survive it, Tom."

He pats my hand. "It's been arranged right from the beginning — your Eorthe parents won't know when she's gone. They won't remember her. Time for them — and all of those who knew her here — will be altered."

"But *she'll* never forget!" I say fiercely. "And I don't believe they could be made to forget her."

"Look — perhaps when the time's right, she could return to Eorthe for short stays. It's even possible that your parents could be told —"

I sneer. "Told what? That both of their children are *changelings?*"

That's when I remember something else. "I *know* Mom gave birth to a child the night Summer was born. I *know* it. So how could — what happened?"

"The Keeper's daughter was chosen to be *your* mother simply because her child died and you were available to be a Pithwitchen. Fergus always puts various youngers of Watchers in different places, just in case he needs them one day. Then some years later, when Summer's family was killed, the Royal Child of Argadnel was brought here — because Fergus and his people knew that *you* would take care of her as she grew. That it was bred into you to watch over her the minute you laid eyes on her."

"So did Mom give birth to her own child that night or not? She was expecting a baby and —" I leap to my feet. "Wait! Do you mean Fergus somehow *killed* Mom's real baby?" I feel as if my head is going to explode on my shoulders. "How could he kill Mom's very own baby and put this —" I point at Summer. "My grandpa MacFey must have known. How could he have been part of this?"

"Yes. He knew. Keepers are the most trustworthy and loyal of folk. That, too, is bred into them. When he was asked to give up his grandchild, he knew the child would go to the other side — through the portal. It's not a punishment, Emma — at least he wouldn't have seen it like that — he'd have felt *honored*."

I remember Grandpa MacFey talking to Ina all those years ago — he'd used those very words, saying his grandchild would be going to a better place.

Tom is still talking. "... then he died and the portal here was forgotten, and no one was sent to replace him, and your mother clearly hadn't been trained to take over from him."

"Wait a minute. Go back — you mean they didn't kill Mom's baby?" I kneel beside Summer. I can't breathe. It's as if someone is stamping the breath out of my lungs.

"No, no, Emma! They didn't kill her. Your parent's Eorthe child is safe and happy, I can promise you that."

"But how do you know?"

"Believe me. I know. The child has grown up — well and healthy."

I shake my head back and forth. "It's wrong. It's all *wrong*."

Tom crouches next to me and puts his hand on my head. It's heavy and comforting, but his next words send a jolt of fear through me.

"Huw will be searching for us," he says solemnly. "We haven't much time, Emma."

I look at the little girl that I know only as my sister. The fear inside me is strong and fierce.

I look up into Tom's gentle, battered face. "And she'll die if she stays here?"

"Yes. She'll die ... soon. If not by the Fading, then by Rhona's command."

I swallow hard. "Will Huw kill her, Tom?"

He shakes his head. "He's a Celtoi. They're allowed to kill only in Game battle. He'll take her back to the queen, and she'll have a ritual death performed."

"And if you can get Summer to the island of Argadnel, my parents — our parents — won't know she's gone until … unless she comes back for a while?"

"Yes. We must take her now, before it's too late. We'll have to bypass everyone else. I don't trust Fergus, Emma. Like I said, if he gets his hands on her, he'll use her in the Game he's set up with Huw and Rhona. He's a volatile and fickle creature. Mathus has kept him under control — however …" He shrugs.

"But will he punish you? He's your boss," I say.

Tom looks at me with amusement. "Boss? Like one of those big-shot corporate kings in your new cities? Yes, I suppose he is. But he can't fire me. I will, however, have to face the Pathfinder's wrath — the one who oversees the Watchers … perhaps a Game tribunal. Fergus will never trust me again. But my loyalties are changed now — a strange feeling. Once we get Summer back where she belongs, I can face what comes afterward. But, Emma, none of this matters if Huw gets to Summer first."

I stand up. "How do we get her to safety?"

32

"We'll have to use all of our powers to avoid Huw," Tom says.

"Powers?"

"You haven't felt them?"

I remember how I hid myself in the cave during my dream and how Huw couldn't see us beside the ice-cream shop. Did I actually make us disappear because I wished it? And when I was in Grandpa MacFey's wood, didn't I smell things I'd never been able to smell before, hear things I'd never heard before — and what about letting the earth direct me out of the maze? And hadn't I flown over the top of the wall of vines into the safety of the cave? Come to think of it — of course — the little creature I'd played in the Fidchell game had exactly the same powers.

I say, "How will I know what to do?"

"A lot of it is instinct — it's been bred into us — but I'll help you. We have to get Summer to the henge and from there to Argadnel — we can't let the others see us. Fergus will soon know I've betrayed them all." He touches my cheek. "To protect you, Creirwy."

"You called me that before. What does it mean?"

"It means ... 'little one,' that's all." His face is flushed.

"And you're doing this for me?"

"And Summer, of course," he says. "But ... you are an unskilled Watcher. You need protecting, too. Tell me this, Emma — you say you played Fidchell with the old man?"

I nod.

"The board game is used as a test, Emma. He knows you have raw unexercised abilities, and now he knows how powerful they are. You've scared them. You've become dangerous to them."

"How?"

"They know that once you realize Summer is in danger, you'll hide her or move her to another world — and make life miserable for them. You're unpredictable. They're waiting only for me to announce the circle gate is ready. Then they'll grab her and go."

"And you haven't told them it's ready. But why do we have to use the portal at all? Can't we just *go*?" I ask.

"Watchers can go without them," he says, "but Summer can't."

I try to draw some air into my lungs but they've shrunk to the size of gumballs.

Tom takes my hands in his. Deep inside his eyes is something I recognize, something old and familiar. The dark brown irises change, growing deep green, ringed with pure white, and his black hair turns pale as moonlight. I feel bodiless, free, light, as if my bones are filled with air, as if I can do anything.

In a soft voice, he whispers, "This day ends together. Don't be afraid."

With that, he picks Summer up, puts one of her arms around his neck and holding her like a baby in the crook of his arm, strides quickly to the door.

"Wait. I can't go without saying good-bye to my parents — to let them know —"

"They won't know you're gone, Emma. And you can come back one day."

"Can you absolutely promise me that they won't know we're gone?"

He hesitates.

"And if I go, can you promise I'll be able to come back?"

Silence.

"You can't promise anything, can you, Tom? I *have* to say good-bye to them. At least *see* them one last time. Please."

Slowly he nods, then says, "As soon as the door opens, Emma, we're at risk. I can hide Summer and myself, but you will not be able to sustain invisibility for long on your own. We will go as far as we can, just as if we're on our way to the market. We'll move directly to your parents' stall. However, when I feel the time is right, you must do what I do, *be* what I tell you to be. You *must*. Even if you haven't seen your parents. Do you understand?"

"But ... how?"

He growls, "Do it!"

I have no idea what he's talking about, but I'm too frightened to argue. Outside, the sun is bright and everything looks normal, but heightened somehow, sharper, clearer.

"We'll slide through the market," he says over his shoulder. "Speak to your parents if you must, but make it brief. If we run into anyone before then, we'll say Summer isn't well and you're taking her to your parents. If we go straight to the henge, we could run the risk of Mathus picking up on your energy anyway, so this is probably the best way to disperse some of it. Just follow my lead."

"Okay." My whole body is vibrating. I think about the Fidchell game. I think about the maze in the forest. I think about my inner powers.

"Emma," he says sharply, "I feel energy careening off you. Calm yourself — otherwise Mathus or Huw *will* know what we're up to."

"Calm myself?" I mutter. "How?"

"*Do* it."

I take a deep breath and think about the quiet of the barn, imagining I'm back on the farm, helping Mom pour honey slowly into hot clear jars. My heart rate goes down.

"Better," Tom says.

We've just made it to the dirt road that leads to the market when he mutters, "Drat and blast it all to Ochain! There's Albert. Well, good thing it's him. Not a speck of ability in that one. Be calm. Give nothing away." He nudges me. "Use your inner eye — direct it above his brow and you may see something of interest."

As we draw near the old green truck, Albert's head pops out of the driver's side window. "Hellooo!" he cries. "Emma! I thought you'd quit on me. Are you coming back?"

I smile at him, but it feels as if my cheeks will crack. "Yeah, sure, I'll be back."

"Oh good," he says, then frowns. "Where are you two off to? Isn't that your sister, Emma? What's wrong with her?"

I try to shrug nonchalantly. "She's tired, that's all. We were walking to the market to help Mom and Dad when Tom came along. As usual, Summer started moaning about tired legs, so he offered to carry her. She fell asleep. Do you need help at your stall?"

"No. I'm doing fine. I'm already out of basil, so I've grabbed someone to hold the fort while I go and pick more." Albert looks at Summer's sleeping form, then at Tom. "You know where your duty lies."

"Yes. I do," Tom says, smiling.

Albert gives a hesitant smile back, before fastening his sharp eyes on me. *What did Tom say about using my inner eye?* I narrow my vision and focus on a spot between Albert's eyebrows. Almost instantly, he dissolves and reshapes into … I try not to squeak out loud … the woman from the field two nights ago. Branwen — Fergus's sister. I blink and she becomes Albert again.

Tom grabs my arm. "See you later, Albert," he calls. The truck pulls slowly away as if Albert is uncertain about leaving.

"That's not Albert," I whisper. "That's Fergus's sister, Branwen."

"Yes."

I stare at Tom. "You mean I really saw her?"

He grins at me.

"And Poppy Maxim? The old man? I saw Fergus in his room yesterday. Is the old man really *Fergus*? In some kind of magical disguise?"

"Mathus is gifted at shape-shifting himself and others. He made Fergus into Poppy Maxim to make sure he stayed put during his most vulnerable times."

"What do you mean?"

"Fergus is at risk between sun height and dusk. Noon to around six o'clock. During that time even Mathus's powers can't help him. Fergus is erratic and sometimes as dangerous to himself as to others when he's so pent up. He's been out of control since Rhona's refusal to side with him against Keir. Now that Mathus has removed the shape-shift off Poppy — Fergus — he'll be anxious to take the child and get out of here."

"Tom —" I begin, but he cuts me off by walking quickly through the crowd of people milling at the entrance to the market. Most stalls are filled with fresh vegetables, some are piled high with jars and bottles of preserves, others cluttered with pies, cakes and bags of cookies. As Tom weaves his way among the squash of buyers, I have to trot to keep up.

"And Janet?" I say, puffing. "There's only one person left — Fergus's Druvid, Mathus!"

Tom doesn't answer but I know I'm right. Still cradling Summer with one arm, he grabs me by the wrist and says, "Your parents are over there. Be quick. Give nothing away. I'll wait here with the child."

He's worried. I glance around. I can't see anything unusual. Yet I can't seem to move. I wonder if I've made a mistake asking him to do this. What can I possibly say to them? Mom will ask where Summer is. When I look across the narrow walkway at my parents' stall, I feel a wave of grief so profound I can't move. My mother is handing a jar of honey to someone in a large straw hat, smiling and nodding, while my father talks animatedly to a couple examining the larger jars filled with thick chunks of honeycomb.

What will they do without us? How can they be made to forget us?

I must have said it out loud, for Tom wraps one arm around me. "We'll make sure they don't suffer your loss, I promise you." Then his arm stiffens. Frightened, I follow his gaze.

The man in the straw hat is looking straight at us. Under the brim's shadow, I see swirling blue tattoos.

33

Everything happens at once. Tom pulls me away as Huw throws his hat to one side and lopes toward us. I register shock on Mom's face and then a horrible recognition as she stares from Tom, Summer and me back to the man she's just served. Tom, with Summer in his arms, races along the line of tents to a short windbreak of dense bushes with me following hard on his heels.

Tom's voice rings inside my head. *Hide! Now! Do it now!* And he vanishes into the windbreak.

I stare at the thick shrubs. How can I get inside there? Something grabs my arm, pulls me hard and before I know it, I'm smack in the middle of a mesh of twigs and branches.

"Tom? Where are you?" I whisper frantically.

"Shhh!" comes a warning close by. "Think it — don't speak it. I'm right here."

All I can see are leaves and thin spiky branches as tightly woven as a blanket. How did I get inside without breaking it to bits? In front of me, a clump of foliage moves and a face of leaves hovers in front of mine, only Tom's eyes recognizable. When I look down, there's nothing but green. I'm not here anymore. Tentatively, I hold up one hand. A mass of dark glistening leaves slides in front of my eyes — leaves that move when I move — that flutter like fingers when I wiggle them.

I've hidden us. You can do the same thing when you want. Tom's voice whispers inside my head. *Don't move. He may pass us by and then we can decide what to do next.* Suddenly his tone grows urgent. *When I say GO, I want you to run to Sweeney's henge. Go to the circle. Stay there. Wait for me. I'll scout from above. Don't be afraid of what you see. You can control it. Here — take Summer. Don't move until I tell you to, then run as fast as you can. Use the trees and bushes to hide.*

"Just like when I played Fidchell."

Whist! Silence.

A rustle of foliage and Summer's slight weight is in my arms. A shadow flutters back and forth in front of the bushes. I peer out and see Huw pacing nearby, hands on hips. Right alongside him is the outline of the watery thing that followed him down Main Street.

Just as Huw raises his hands to part the bushes, something stops him. He spins around. Mom is right in his face, shouting, "Who are you? Why are you chasing my daughters? Who was that boy? Where are my girls!"

GO! Tom's voice is loud inside my head.

I hesitate. Mom needs help.

He won't harm her. Go! Now!

I swirl through the stand of bushes and erupt on the other side, Summer as light as a bag of leaves in my arms. Tom zips past us and runs ahead through a small open pasture. One of Albert's herb fields is on the other side of this meadow, then a bee field ringed with bushes where I can hide from Huw. With luck, Mom will distract him long enough for the three of us to get to the henge. As I run, leaves flutter from me like green snow.

I keep my eyes on Tom. I've never moved so fast in my life, my feet barely brushing the ground. I feel just like I did playing Fidchell — light and fast, as if I could fly without actually trying. Ahead of me, Tom doesn't even leave footprints in the dirt, but suddenly his whole body shudders and changes, legs and feet vanish, and he's off the ground — flying! — like a small plane leaving the local airfield. He soars straight up, and when he turns and flies back over me, I recognize my barn owl.

His voice is as clear as a microphone in my head. *Don't stop. Keep on to the henge. I'll go back and see where Huw is!*

I feel the wind under his wings ruffle my hair and then he's gone. I run full tilt at the fence, tuck my legs up under me, soar over it, hit the ground on the other side and crash right into Albert. Basil plants fly everywhere. Holding Summer tight to my chest, I keep running.

"What the —" Albert lunges after me. His bony fingers cut into my arm and I trip and fall.

Struggling, I gasp, "Huw — he wants Summer. I have to —"

He lets me go. "Huw? He's here? He breached the circle gate? I have to tell Fergus. Take her to the henge. We'll meet you there."

He runs across the field and suddenly he becomes Branwen, long hair streaming out behind. I call out to her, but she shatters into a swarm of tiny lights and vanishes.

We'll meet you there, she said. Now I have to beat her, Mathus *and* Fergus to the henge as well. I search the sky for Tom as I run across the field. Should I run for home? No, I can't. Summer's too sick. Tom says she has to go to her island in the other world or she'll die.

I *have* to go to the henge.

I race straight across the herb field and when I reach the meadow of beehives, I run into the ring of bushes without hesitation and keep running. I must keep hidden. I can hear a low humming that seems to come right through the ground into my toes. Is it the bees? I reach the henge field and push aside a screen of leaves.

The circle stands shimmering in the late-morning sunshine, the oak tree casting its black shadow across the main opening to the henge. Tom instructed me to wait at the circle. Did he mean in the middle of it? I can't remember exactly what he said. I run across the field into the circle, lower Summer to the ground and check the socle, hoping to remove the amethyst I left there last night in case Tom needs it. But it's not there.

A creeping anxiety starts in my toes and slides slowly up my spine. Heart thumping in my ears, I lean down to scoop my sleeping sister into my arms. Someone's watching me. I can *feel* it right through my skin. Why didn't I stay hidden in the bushes until Tom came? If I can just make it back to that leafy hiding place.

But I'm too late.

From inside the oak's shadow, the undulating shape that was following Huw slides toward us. I gather Summer close to me, close my eyes and wish a box of protection around us. When I open them, the thing is sliding like glistening jelly around the outside of an invisible wall. Did I construct the box with my mind? I hold tightly to the image of a glass cage and glare fiercely at the thing crawling around the outside.

A disembodied laugh nearby makes my heart stop. Then a voice says, "Well, my little one, you're the child's Watcher, mmm? It's easy to see they made the right choice. You've created an excellent protective case, useless though it will be to you in the end."

It's Keir. I recognize his weird choked voice.

The thing slides off the invisible wall. As it does, a figure forms like a negative turning into a photograph, and a tall, strong-legged man appears. He has a large narrow head, hooked nose and thick thatch of silver hair. One of his eyes is bluish and cloudy, the other smaller and shiny as a green marble. His skin has a curious blue tinge. He's encased in a shell of greeny-gold that looks like snakeskin. His right hand looks normal, but his left is scaly and a deep bloodless gray, a thick jeweled band strapped around its wrist.

I blurt out, "But you don't look the same. You're not that monster in the silver cart."

"You saw me then? Got through the cunning lock all on your own, did you? Won't Mathus be *raging* when he finds out!" He looks down at himself. "Aaah, yes. I see what you mean. It's taken me some time to re-animate here, as I don't have Huw's skills. I was becoming quite perturbed that I'd remain unformed. But lo and regard, here I am! Best of all, it appears that coming to this land has temporarily released me of Mathus's cunning spell." His laugh is a deep growling sneer. "As to Huw, he's a bumpkin!

I hitched a ride with him when he came through, and he didn't even know I was in the cave!"

Despite my fear, I croak, "Where is he?"

"I left that cretinous bungler tangling with a woman and followed you." His eyes narrow shiftily, and he shows a row of pointed teeth in a short-lipped leer that reminds me of that horrible fish in the black glass door. "Now — let me have the child and I won't harm you, Watcher."

I clutch Summer tighter and shake my head. "No."

Keir's arm drops swiftly to his side, and when he lifts it, he holds a long pointed dart that flashes like a sparkler in his thick blue fingers.

"Replace it, Keir, or you will be struck down," a voice bellows.

Fergus stands at the base of the oak, Mathus on one side, Branwen on the other. All three are armed with long feathered darts.

Keir's face twists with rage, but then he laughs harshly and in one movement he puts his weapon into a jeweled strap around his waist.

"The child's of no consequence, Fergus," he says. "The island kingdom is mine."

Fergus snorts. "Playing the fool, Keir, as always." He looks at me crouched by the table, Summer tightly guarded by my body. "So, here we are, Sparrow, you and I — playing Fidchell for real. You've exercised the Game well, but we'll take her now. Your job is over."

I recognize Poppy Maxim's voice, and the man's black eyes glitter with a reckless malevolence I recognize from playing Fidchell.

As bravely as I can, I reply, "You can't have her."

Fergus flaps his hand at me and casually announces, "Mathus, break the protective wall. The child is ours."

Mathus shakes his head. "I can't, sire. She's too powerful."

Fergus stares at him. "What? That bit of a thing? Don't be ridiculous!"

"We'll have to wait for her to drop her defenses. But if she —"

"Do it!" Fergus snarls, and looks murderously at Keir, who laughs loud and long.

"A slip of a Watcher has you both bamboozled," he crows. "Perhaps, little Watcher, you'll agree to some rare and wonderful tokens in exchange for the child? I can promise you many things."

"Never!" My voice is a whistle of wind in my ears — high and fierce.

Keir looks puzzled — then comes close to the clear wall and gazes at me, his strange eyes blinking slowly — assessing, planning.

"Keir," Fergus says, "if you go back to Fomorii — with or without the child — you'll once again be the prisoner of that beast cunning. If you leave now, forfeit this prize and agree to never claim Argadnel, I'll have Mathus remove the cunning from you. Forever."

"Hmm. What do *you* say to that generous offer, Huw?" Keir calls to the man who has suddenly appeared in the henge.

Huw, ignoring Keir's heckling, strides toward me. "You'll release this child to no one but me."

"Looks like she's not about to pass it to anyone," Keir growls. "And as Rhona isn't here, I'm in charge."

Huw sneers at him. "I promised your queen I'd bring the heir to Argadnel to her. She'll never give you the island kingdom now that you've come here without her consent. And I won't let you get in my way even if I, too, have to put a cunning on you."

"My queen will never forgive you if you dare such a thing!" Keir roars, his face black with fury.

Fergus says, "Take my offer, Keir. This game is at a deadlock because of this younger. She doesn't know her place yet. But we'll break her even if we have to stay here until the child fades completely. Rhona will never have this child. The island will never be yours." He looks over at me. "It may never be the child's, either."

What does he mean? That Summer will die? What should I do now? Where's Tom?

"Well, Keir?" he says.

Keir takes a deep breath. "Yes ... why not? Perhaps I'll linger here for a while. There's probably all sorts of kingdoms lying fallow that I can take as my own. It's an old world, untapped for eons. I could build up an army of players. Yes, why not?"

Fergus says, "It's all yours. Mathus, remove the beast cunning."

Mathus is clearly unhappy with the order. As he hesitates, Summer stirs in my arms. "No. Please don't wake up. Not now! Not yet!" I whisper.

Mathus flicks his hand and a film of light slides over Keir. At the same time, Huw's bony arm rises into the air and swings down again like a weighted pendulum. Mom appears at the edge of the row of trees and as she runs toward us, I feel my grip on the wall of protection crumble.

And somewhere in that flash of time, Summer vanishes from my arms.

34

A terrible silence hangs in the henge as if a loud bell has suddenly stopped ringing. Mom, arms held tight by Branwen, stares at something in the air. So do the others, except for Huw, a curved grin on his hawk face. I look up. A large moth with long trailing wings of the palest green flutters above our heads.

"It's mine," Huw whispers hoarsely in the silence. "I have it in my cunning eye. If you try to stop it coming to me, Mathus, I'll kill it."

The moth's flight is hesitant, dipping and rising in the still air as if it's losing its strength and will soon fall to the ground. Huw speaks to it in a low mesmerizing chant. The moth lifts higher and drifts toward his upturned palm.

"Emma?" Mom cries. "Where is she? Where's Summer?"

The late-morning sky is dark now, the light hazy, a heavy blue cast over everything. Even the sounds, like Mom's voice, have altered, seeming far away and muffled. The moth bobs uncertainly through the air, passes over Huw and floats toward Mom.

"To me!" Huw commands, his words dull and muted. Once again the delicate creature changes course.

Mathus slides in front of Huw, lifts one arm as if he's throwing a ball and pitches something at the moth, which drops to the ground and reshapes into a small yellow mouselike creature that sits frozen for a moment, then skitters frantically through the grass. In the hush, I can hear its faint chirruping squeaks.

Suddenly, there's a heavy cracking sound and Mathus is thrown to one side, as if he's been hit. He struggles to his feet and raises his fist. The two Druvids stand like gunfighters ready to draw. Keir lunges at the frightened mouse with lightning speed and is about to snatch it up when, from nowhere, the barn owl swoops into the circle, glides neatly under his arm, lifts the tiny creature in his talons and flies away, wings beating slowly … too slowly, like he's flying through water, not air. I will him to pick up speed. Keir's arm moves in a wide arc and something whirs past my face. The next moment, the owl twists in the air and drops straight down onto the top of the socle.

"Tom!" I cry, but my voice reverberates back to me in the thick air.

He lies half on his side, not moving, his eyes wide open in surprise, Summer unhurt in his arms. Mom runs to her, lifts her off the table, edges away from the five people moving toward her and backs into one of Dad's Plexiglas stones. She stares at me, eyes wide with fear.

"Emma," she croaks, "Emma ..."

We need to get away. But we can't go without Tom. They'll punish him for what he's done. Why doesn't he move?

"Tom?" I whisper. "Tom?" Only when I get close do I see the jeweled dart embedded deep in his chest. He blinks once, looks at me and smiles. "Creirwy," he whispers, before releasing a long deep sigh.

He — he can't be dead. He can't be!

Fergus's hand appears over my shoulder. He touches Tom's neck, then looks questioningly at Mathus. "Damnation!" he growls. "Not a Watcher! The Pathfinder's response will be fierce. It'll resonate throughout the Game. Can't you do anything, Mathus?"

Mathus shakes his head and in a flat voice says, "I have no power over Watchers. They're strange singular beings."

I'm mesmerized by a thin line of Tom's blood as it runs along the surface of the altar's top — soon it will be soaking into the ground below. Somehow I know I can't let it land on Eorthe's soil. I cup one hand to catch the single warm drop that falls.

"On a crystal altar they'll lay him, with his spilt blood all around, and one will catch it in a palm, ere it reach the ground …," a melodic voice says right beside me. "It's a good thing I arrived before he blocked the way through. I thought it would be a warrior who died — not a Watcher. Too bad it's Tamhas. He was quite gifted."

I look up into the blue-tinged face of Rhona, Queen of Fomorii. A thin green vaporous light glitters all around her. She's dressed like her brother, but her tight second skin is a glistening opalescent green. Over her shoulders and lacquered hair is a puffed hood covered in spikes like a sea urchin, scattered with pure white pearls. Silver shells tinkle on her wrists.

"Please," I whisper. "Don't let them harm my sister. Don't let Tom die."

She offers me a chilly smile and shrugs. "What makes you think I can change anything, my dear? I have only just arrived." She has the same eyes as her brother, one milky and dead looking, the other a dark intense green. Her left hand is a scaly bloodless gray and has a thick jeweled band at the wrist, like Keir's. She runs one gray finger over the socle and thin blue sparks fizz in the air. Then she looks around and says, "Why has the Game stopped? I expected to arrive in time to enjoy a good skirmish."

Huw bows and points at me. "Madam, this young Watcher has thrown off the rhythm of the Game."

"But why? How?" She gives me an assessing look of icy coldness.

"She's the Watcher of the child. Has had no training. Stopped us in our tracks."

"Really! How very interesting." She looks at me for one more second, then turns and walks in her stiff-legged gait toward the people in the circle. Behind her head, the silver hood narrows and drops straight down her back, trailing along the ground like a spiked slender tail. Shells tinkle in the muffled stillness.

She stops in front of her brother and in a low voice says, "So, you've disobeyed me for the last time, Keir. You won't return to Fomorii. I strip you of your title and all inheritances." She hands him a small bag. "Gold for a traitor."

Keir takes the bag and grins at her. "Oh, you'll forgive me, my dear heart — in time. I *am* your blood. Still, I can enjoy myself in this world for quite some time. When you miss me, send your messenger."

She turns away from him. He smirks and strides across the field and in a scattering of light, disappears into Grandpa MacFey's wood.

Huw says, "The child is there for the taking, my queen."

"No!" Mom's voice ripples through the circle henge. "You can't take her! She's my daughter!"

Rhona offers her a chilly smile. "But she's not, you see. That's why we're all here. This child belongs to me."

Fergus laughs. "You are sadly mistaken, madam."

Summer asks, "What do they mean, Mom? What do they mean?"

Mom's voice is hoarse. "Emma, come here. We're going home."

I look at the single drop of blood on my palm and then at Tom's closed, silent face. The pain inside me is desperate and raw. I touch the drop with my fingertip and trace a line through the crescent moons on my wrist and, turning his wrist toward me, I slide a copper bracelet off his arm and run a smear of red across the stars and moon on his still-warm skin. The red streak turns a pale green and vanishes. I look at my own wrist. No sign of red there, either.

"Now we are the same blood," I whisper. I slide his bracelet onto my own wrist.

"Emma!" Mom's voice wraps around me. At the same time, I hear the low droning of bees.

I stumble into the circle of her arm. I can feel her shaking — or is it me? Blocked by Dad's Plexiglas stone, we have no way out. The others surround us. Locked together, we watch Rhona turn her attention to Fergus.

He smiles insolently and bows.

"So, we meet after all this time. I vowed I would destroy you if I saw you again," she hisses. "But, here without my players, it would lose its panache, its ... satisfaction."

"As a warrior you are unequaled, madam. No doubt I should die simply by looking at the icy daggers in your eyes."

They gaze at each other, and a crackling energy arcs across the space between them.

"Now that we are here in this godforsaken place, it hardly seems …," Rhona begins and waves her hand casually at the henge circle.

One side of Fergus's mouth lifts slightly. "Worth it? My people and I have been here for two moon crossings and I am ready to return to Cleave. Now that you have punished your brother, we can perhaps … still, there *is* the child, isn't there? If she fades, and her people find out that I could have saved her, well … that would not be a game I particularly relish, as the folk of Argadnel are coarse and unrefined players and could menace us for many moon crests. Perhaps you and I can agree to a middle ground?"

Mathus clears his throat loudly. Huw takes two steps toward his mistress, who lifts a slender hand and stops him.

"A middle ground?" she asks, one eyebrow raised.

"You allow me to return the child to her kingdom and I won't take full control of how she rules it. You can choose someone from your people to represent her interests and I'll choose a Watcher to be *my* representative. We'll let her own council choose someone to keep an eye on everyone else. Then every faction will be happy and we could move on to a game more worthy of our skills."

"And if I don't agree?"

"We'll be at war — here and now," Fergus says. "I have just lost my favored Watcher. You owe me for that. It was your kin who extinguished him."

"And that makes this game a draw, is that what you think? That now we're even?" Rhona says scornfully.

He shakes his head. "Madam, we'll *never* be even. And we'll always misunderstand each other. It's our destiny. But that's what makes all of this so ... exhilarating."

"If I go along with you, who will you choose as the child's Watcher?" she asks. Glancing at me, she adds, "Or should I ask? But she will have to be trained."

Fergus nods. "Perhaps you will walk with me for a moment and we can strike a pact?"

She looks at him with level eyes and says, "Perhaps. A short lull before our game begins again?" She turns and together they walk around the outside of Dad's henge.

Mathus looks at Huw and shakes his head. "Those two will forever clash spirits and swords."

Huw smiles grimly and shrugs. "Either way, you and I will have the cleaning up to do afterward. If they come to an agreement, the child will go to Argadnel. If they don't, the game will resume with even more intensity."

I cry, "It's all just a stupid game! For what? *Why?*"

Branwen turns to me and cries, "Oh, Emma, to win, of course! But please, don't be angry. I so enjoyed our time together." Her eyes have Albert's warmth. Maybe ...

"Can't you help us somehow?" I beg her.

"No, sadly I can't, dear Emma. Fergus won't change his mind. He hates stalemates, compromises — and if it was anyone but Rhona, well ... As for Rhona, she's no different. Both suffer defeat badly. For now, though, the child will come with all of us. You can come, too. And perhaps we can be friends. For a while. Until a new game begins."

"Never," I hiss.

I feel the strength of my mother's arm tighten. "No one is taking my kids anywhere. Not without killing me first." She closes her eyes tight. The low drone in the distance intensifies, and suddenly the sky is swarming with bees that come together, creating a clouded dome over the henge.

Mathus looks up, smiles and bows. "Madam, I'm impressed. But killing you won't be necessary, I assure you."

Huw adds in a sneering tone, "You're the daughter of the Keeper of the Fourth Border Circle. You must know these two ... beings ... are not yours."

"No! It's not true. I gave birth to Summer. I heard her cry. I held her in my arms. They're mine. I won't give them up."

"But ... even then as you heard the child cry, you knew something was wrong, didn't you?" Mathus asks gently. "Eorthe mothers always know. Uncanny, but true."

Mom shakes her head back and forth and says stubbornly, "They're my daughters. They're *my* children."

The swarm of bees lowers, the sound deafening.

She gazes up at them and starts to raise her arms, but Huw's voice is sharp and loud. "Be careful, madam. I will destroy them in an instant. Don't threaten us!"

"No one takes my children from me," Mom says, her voice shaking, her eyes fierce.

I push in front of her. "No one harms my family!" I shout.

Mathus laughs loudly, turns to Huw and says, "What better representative could the young queen have than two creatures who are interested only in her well-being. After all, the woman is clearly the daughter of the Keeper. And it's said this young Watcher comes from the Source of Aibell and Clust." He looks at Mom, at me and at the little girl in our protective circle and says, "Perhaps, my dear ladies, we, too, can negotiate a pact?"

Epilogue

I can't believe it's been more than an Earth month since we were brought to Argadnel. I'm sitting curled up on a high branch in a tall tree — well, it's not a tree exactly, but close enough — at the edge of a silver sea, watching Mom and Summer. The island, called Silver Cloud by travelers and Recorders, usually stands high above the ocean on a silver pillar, but for about one hour a day, it's lowered so that Summer (now the little Queen Elen) can play on the shore. She has been given a small gray puppy — one of the offspring of Rhona's hounds. His feet are huge and webbed, his ears flopping all over his narrow head. He's splashing through the water and Summer is running up and down on the sparkling white sand, shrieking with delight. She's grown taller in the short time she's been here, and with her long, straight black hair she's looking less like Mom and more like her own people — who are very tall and slender with black hair and fierce, intense eyes. Eyes that watch her every move. These include the pale blue eyes of Rhona's emissary, Bedeven, a small man with a flat expression that doesn't give away a single thought. He seems to be everywhere at once. I don't trust him for one second.

Sitting on the sand on a low seat, Mom watches Summer play. Mom smiles now and again, but there is a deep sadness in those rare smiles. As Summer grows willowy and strong, Mom seems to waste away. She's missing Dennis — Dad — and I don't know how to fix it. Does he remember us? Would he agree to come back here? I might be able to find my way to him and I could take Mom, but I'm afraid I'd lose her along the way — or land in some other world I've never been before. I'm not confident enough in my skills to risk her life. In a short while I'm to go off to where the Pathfinder resides to learn the powers of a real Watcher, but I can't wait that long to get Mom and Dad together again. I fear she'll die without him. She's skin and bones, and her hair is fully gray now. She tries to be cheerful but she's barely half of herself. She and Dad are meant to be together. She also knows now that her birth child is out there somewhere, and I know she's hoping I'll find her someday.

I rub my hand over my head and feel the cap of fine white hair. Today I'm Emma. At least I look like her. It's almost funny at times. Sometimes I forget to be Emma, and when I catch my image in a looking glass, I see the pale creature with the crest of white hair and I jump inside myself — for I don't know who that creature really is. I look like something from a book about Ye Olde Faerie Creatures or something. I'm getting a little more used to seeing her, but most of the time I stay in my comfortable, familiar Emma body. For now, at least.

But I *do* know who I am inside. I'm a Watcher. That was imprinted on me the moment I was formed. My purpose, according to Branwen — who I see all the time now — is clear. She says I'm a Watcher and only a Watcher, and I can't change who I am. But I can't accept this imprint as my complete self. I accept my role as Watcher — I embrace it — but thanks to Mom and Dad, I know that I also have free will. Does that make me human? How human am I? I don't know yet. I do know that I watch over Mom and Summer, not because I'm programmed to but because I love them. I know what love is. I know what it's like to have all the mixed-up irrational feelings that are human. I know how painful it is to miss someone. I know how hard it is to lose someone forever.

Branwen would laugh if she heard me. She's the representative of Fergus's faction — I refused to be — and lives on the island. I chose to be the agent of the people of Argadnel. That way I'm on the side I want to be on — Summer's. I don't trust Branwen any more than I trust Bedeven, Rhona's representative, but I'm growing to like her more and more. She was left here when Mathus and Huw delivered us to the island. They moved on soon after in an airship — the last I saw of them, they were laughing together as the vessel rose from Argadnel's port.

They don't know — and neither does Branwen — that I've discovered a border cave on the island. I sat at its entrance looking down at the sea far below and for just a moment, the scene split in two and a monstrous city formed on my right — all whirls and swirling rounded peaks and unbelievable colors. I have no idea where this place is. I was so frightened by its size that I raced for home.

Mom talked to me once about being in a borderland between childhood and adulthood. How simple it would have been to be a human growing up. The borderlands I'll have to face are beyond anything she and I ever dreamed of.

I'm scared all the time. Scared for Mom. For Summer. For the future. I have no idea how the Game will affect our lives here on Argadnel. I have so many decisions to make. And I feel so alone.

I miss Tom.

I know he'd guide me through this. I know he'd agree to help me bring Dad here. I wish I was back in the barn overlooking the familiar farmhouse. If only I could sit on the beam in the barn and wait for the owl's return. If only I'd understood then what I know now, I might have been able to save him — save Tom. I look at the copper bracelet on my wrist. I remember the blood that floated into my veins and back into his dying body. And I remember his

words, *Think of me — I mean really* think *about me ...*
I see him running across the field, I see him taking
off in flight ... I see his kind, lovely, ugly face, his
strong back ...

I lean my head against the branch and close my
eyes to cut off the tears. I hear a wuffting sound
like the beating of soft wings against a window. I
look up and my heart stops.

Sitting on a nearby branch gazing at me is a large
white owl with a heart-shaped face.

About the Author

It took almost 30 years for Margaret Buffie to become a writer. "My father told me how much he would like me to be an artist," she says. "He died when I was 12, and I treasured the memories of his praise and honored his wishes. I became an artist."

Buffie received a degree in fine art from the University of Manitoba in 1967 and, shortly afterwards, married fellow artist Jim Macfarlane. After graduating, she worked as an illustrator before obtaining a teaching certificate in 1976. For the next two years, Buffie taught high school art and continued as a freelance illustrator. She also exhibited many of her own oil paintings in Winnipeg.

One day, Buffie began reading some of her 12-year-old daughter's books. "I found that the writing was astoundingly good, and I suddenly had the urge to write."

Buffie began by writing a journal describing her father's last illness, her mother's struggle to hold down two jobs in order to make the mortgage payments, and Buffie's effort to find her own identity among three strong-willed sisters. "It was when I was writing this journal that I realized how hard those years had been for all of us, and how lonely and frightened I'd been during so much of them."

To explore her themes, Buffie uses the supernatural as her impetus. "I don't believe that great lives die," she says. "There is a link between generations — characteristics passed on and stories told — and I explore those links. I know that when I sit down to write, I will have to explore my brain's ghostly side."

Also by Margaret Buffie

Angels Turn Their Backs

Fifteen-year-old Addy does well in school and adores reading, old movies and needlework. But suddenly, her parents split up, and Addy and her mom move away, leaving behind Addy's school, her father, and her one real friend.

Even when she was a child, Addy was fearful, but now she is falling apart. She can't hear people when they're right in front of her; yet, she hears strange voices and senses a ghostly presence. The world has become hostile, and the only safe place is her apartment in a ramshackle Winnipeg house.

Addy is terrified. She feels as if she's going crazy ... and can't see any way back to the normal world.

Come spend a little time in Addy's head. Your world will change forever.

"The author masterfully weaves diverse elements into a flowing and believable first-person narrative, leaving the reader feeling that one has discovered a special friend."

— *NAPRA*

Also by Margaret Buffie

The Dark Garden

Thea is struggling to discover who she is - and who she is not. Amnesia has robbed her of the past and, as she tries to recover her identity, the empty places of her mind fill up with memories. But whose memories are they? Is she living someone else's terrible dream? Thea begins to hear voices no one else can hear and see people no one else can see.

Thea finds herself caught between two worlds. In one, her unhappy family seems to be falling apart. In the other, shadowy spirits haunt her with their tragic passion. In both there is anger and loneliness, but in the spirit's world there is also murder.

The bridge between the two worlds is a large garden, where time and place, love and hate become blurred — and where anything is possible.

"A first-rate blend of a ghost story and problem novel. Buffie creates a tightly knit, evocatively written, and lushly romantic thriller." — *Kirkus Reviews*

"An exciting and mysterious story, this is a great book."

— *American Bookseller*

IS 61 LIBRARY

DATE DUE
